Maria's Search

Maria's Search

Carole Gift Page

MOODY PRESS
CHICAGO

To my dear friend Sandra Miller,
who was always there for me in
our growing-up years

ISBN: 0-8024-8452-2

1 2 3 4 5 6 Printing/LC/Year 94 93 92 91

Printed in the United States of America

1

Maria Estrella and her father, José, chugged through the red-brown rock world of Arizona's Navajo country in their olive-green Plymouth. Sixteen-year-old Maria sat stiffly, her lips pressed together in mute despair. She was a trim, small-boned girl with her father's dark Colombian features and her mother's Irish red cast in her long black hair.

Maria stared out the window as slanting rain made the landscape blur and shimmer with an ethereal distortion. The whole world seemed to reflect her own bleak mood. Aimless clumps of sagebrush rolled like whirling dervishes beside the road. Ticky-tacky houses drooped in lifeless fields. And on the horizon—mirroring her own deep despondency—dark rocks raged up from the flat, wet belly of the earth like ancient pillars, slick and ominous, veined with ridges and gullies. *A ghostly moonscape,* thought Maria, *as dead as I feel inside.*

Just before they reached the little town of Chinle, the first fragile rays of sunshine glinted through the sky's gray wash. Maria's father pulled into a Shell service station where Indians were clustered around, visiting leisurely. Old men sat stooped on the walk by the men's room while several women in babushkas and full skirts chatted nearby. No one seemed in a hurry. Probably they had nowhere to go. It struck Maria that she too had nowhere to go, nowhere she wanted to go. But her father was taking her just the same. She had protested loudly and often over the past two weeks, demanding of her father, "Why are you dumping me? Why are you leaving again?"

His answer was always the same—abrupt, tight-lipped, as if to say more would open the doors to his own pain. "I have to leave you, Maria. For now anyway. It's settled. Accept it."

But Maria would never accept this new turn her life had taken. Hadn't she suffered enough already, nursing her mother through two tormented years of cancer? Why—now that her mother was dead—should Maria be expected to endure more losses—her father, her home, all that was familiar and secure?

Maria realized suddenly that two young men in wide-brimmed hats, slouching by the gas pumps, were eyeing her with closed, cryptic stares. She shrank down in her seat and was relieved when her father climbed back into the car. "The man says we shouldn't miss Canyon de Chelly National Monument," her father said. "What do you say?"

Maria shrugged. "If you want to." So far today they had left behind forgettable little towns with names like Round Rock, Many Farms, and Mexican Water.

Her father turned the question back to her. "What do you want?"

She wanted to say, *Go home to Colorado,* but the argument was old and threadbare now. What good would it do to rehash it again?

"We'll never get to California if we stop at every tourist attraction," she mumbled. Not that she had the slightest desire ever to reach California!

Her father pulled back onto the highway with a determined, veering motion. "I talked to your grandmother on the phone last night. She said she's looking forward to having you stay with her," he said, as if they had been talking about Grandma Estrella all along.

"I hardly remember her," Maria said sullenly.

"When you were little you were very fond of her. You called her *Abuelita*—Little Grandmother, remember?"

"She always talked in Spanish," said Maria.

Her father gave her a quick, sidelong glance. His thick brows shadowed his small, black eyes. "It's her way of holding on to the old ways. You used to think it was a special, private language between you two.''

"I pretended I understood everything she said," remembered Maria.

"Your grandmother's a wonderful, devout woman, Maria." Her father's voice was gravelly, like the pavement beneath their tires. Maria looked over at him. He was a big, strong man, not quite forty, with square hands and prominent features. His skin was brown and weather-toughened, but his eyes held a perennial moistness, as if he were forcing back unshed tears.

Maria swallowed a lump in her throat. Since her mother's death, she and her father had remained awkward and unspeaking, but their grief flowed together like two streams joining to form a surging river. Why was it so hard to talk about something that never left their minds for a moment? If they didn't talk soon, it would be too late. Spurred on by that sober realization, Maria broke the silence with, "It won't help, you know. It won't change anything.''

"What won't?" her father asked, sounding suspicious.

"Leaving me with Grandma Estrella." Maria took a breath and plunged on. "You want to forget these past two years. You want to forget Mama and all her pain. You think if you send me away, you will forget."

"No," he protested, his knuckles blanching as he gripped the steering wheel. "Nothing under heaven will make me forget—or *let* me forget." His voice grew ragged. "I see your mother's ravaged face—I see her dying inch by inch before my eyes, day after day." He thumped his barrel chest with his fist. "It's etched here, like a scar, always.''

"But don't you see? It will be worse if we are apart."

"There is no choice, Maria. I must work.''

"Can't you get a different job so you don't have to travel so much?''

"What else do I know except selling farm machinery?''

"I could stay home alone while you're gone. I wouldn't mind.''

"But *I* would mind. Since your mother died, I worry every time I have to leave you alone. We both know it isn't safe.''

"But when will I see you?''

"I'll visit you at your grandmother's."

"When?"

"As often as I can."

Maria silently weighed her options, then questioned, "Couldn't you persuade your company to change your territory to the West Coast?"

Her father heaved a sigh. "I doubt it, Maria."

In a last, desperate effort, Maria suggested, "Let me travel with you, Papa. I could put off school for a while, or I could study on my own. I wouldn't be any trouble . . . "

"No, Maria, no!"

She could tell she had pushed her father too far this time, but still she asked in a small voice, "Why not?"

"Because I live out of a suitcase. I sleep in second-class motels. I eat in greasy restaurants. That's no life for a sixteen-year-old girl. You need roots, a stable home."

"I had that," Maria murmured. She shifted her position. Her denim skirt stuck to the plastic seat covers.

"And you'll have a home again," said her father, "with your grandmother."

"But not with you."

"No, Maria," he said as if the argument had exhausted him. "Not with me."

Maria felt exhausted, too. She put her head back and closed her eyes. In spite of the recent downpour, the early July weather was humid and the inside of the car stifling. It appeared to Maria that her course was unalterably set—a strange, new life in a Hispanic barrio of East Los Angeles with a grandmother she scarcely remembered.

2

Early the next afternoon, Maria's father pulled up beside a small yard with sunburned grass and patches of fuzz-yellow dandelions. Maria shuddered with apprehension. Grandmother Estrella's house was worse than she remembered—a boxy, wood-frame structure with peeling paint and a sagging porch. The windows were small with faded curtains and torn screens. It was nothing like the simple but attractive apartment Maria had left behind in Colorado.

Maria cast a doubtful glance at her father and was surprised to read the same troubled expression in his eyes. But as soon as their gaze met, he forced a grin and said cheerily, "Well, let's go in. Your grandmother has probably been watching for us for hours."

Sure enough. Even before they stepped out of the automobile, the screen door squeaked open and Grandma Estrella hobbled out onto the porch with an eager smile. She looked older than Maria expected. She was a squat, ample woman with gentle eyes, a round, leathery face, and stubby, work-worn hands. Her Mexican and Colombian heritage was evident in her caramel coloring and deeply carved features. *"José! Hijo mio!"* she cried as she embraced Maria's father.

Then she opened her arms to Maria. Her skin was soft and rippling and smelled faintly of lavender soap. "Ah, *niña bonita*, you are so grown up, so beautiful!"

Maria allowed herself to be embraced, but she couldn't respond with the warmth her grandmother displayed. She felt as if she were hugging a stranger.

"Come inside," Grandma Estrella told Maria excitedly. "I have fresh tortillas and frijoles and—"

"And a big pitcher of sun tea?" asked Maria's father, wiping his forehead with his handkerchief.

"You remember." Grandma Estrella laughed.

"How could I forget? From the time I was a little boy you always had a jug of sun tea sitting out on the back porch. Papa always said nothing quenches thirst better on a hot day."

Maria had hoped it would be cooler inside, but the small living room was airless, the walls too close, oppressive. The furniture was worn and overstuffed, with a nubby maroon fabric. *Ugly!* thought Maria. The wood floor was covered with a braided, multi-colored rug. On one wall hung a calendar with a mountain scene, on the opposite wall a plaster crucifix. Beneath it, on a narrow buffet sat a ceramic Madonna, her hands crossed gracefully on her breast, her face downcast, serene.

Maria's eyes lingered admiringly on the delicate statue, then settled on the old, upright piano against the far wall. That piano was Maria's favorite memory of Grandma Estrella's home. Maria still recalled sitting happily beside Grandpa Estrella as he banged out energetic tunes on the keys. How she had longed to play as he played. He sang, too, in a deep, booming voice and always urged her to sing along. She had tried in her hesitant, girlish voice, but the Spanish lyrics were strange to her, too difficult to pronounce.

Thinking of Grandfather Estrella, Maria felt a momentary pang of loss. He was gone just like her beloved mother. *Dead.* Good things never lasted long. She'd already learned that—the hard way.

"The old place looks the same," her father was saying as they filed into the narrow kitchen. He opened the small refrigerator and peered inside.

"Always you go first to the icebox." Grandma Estrella chuckled.

"Habit," mused José. "And curiosity. I wanted to take a peek at all the goodies you got in store for us."

"Maybe not so many as before," she lamented. "I don't get out so much these days."

"What's the problem, Mama? Your arthritis?"

"*Sí.* Is worse every day. I try to keep up with my house, but the legs—they don't work like they should."

José turned to the rusty sink and put his hand under the dripping faucet. "Don't worry, Mama. I'll take care of things before I leave."

Grandma Estrella smiled. "You are a good son, José."

José winked. "You just need a man around to fix the plumbing and repair the broken steps and torn screens. Got any candidates, Mama?"

"No one match your papa," she said, "except you, my son."

José fondly squeezed her shoulder, then walked over to the window and looked out. "Mama, did you know your window is broken?"

"*Sí.* The boys down the street—they get crazy sometimes. They make noise . . . break things."

"Gang fights?" José asked. "Did you call the police, report them?"

"I don't want no trouble, José. I mind my own business."

José scowled. "This neighborhood wasn't like that when I was a boy."

Maria sat down at the tiny, oilcloth-covered table. Maybe, if her father saw how poor living conditions were here, he would decide she shouldn't stay. "If it isn't so safe around here," she remarked, "maybe we should pack up Grandma Estrella and take her back to Colorado with us."

"No, no, *niña*," protested her grandmother. "This is Papa's home. I die here."

"We have no home in Colorado anymore, Maria," said her father abruptly. "Besides, I promised Burdwick Manufacturing I'd be free to travel. In fact, I've got to be back at work by the first of next week."

"You must go so soon, José?"

"Yes, Mama. But don't look so sad. You will have Maria to keep you company and help you around the house. She is a good worker."

"Ah, Jose, she is young and pretty and full of life. She will not want to be bothered with a helpless old woman."

"You aren't helpless, Mama. You are strong inside."

"You see only what you want to see, my son."

Jose slipped his arm around his mother. "If the arthritis is so bad, how do you shop, Mama? How do you get what you need?"

"Enrique, a neighbor boy, brings my groceries. I give him money and a little extra for himself."

"Well, now Maria can shop for you," said Jose. "Can't you, Maria?"

Maria nodded automatically, her eyes downcast. She had a sudden, sickening feeling in the pit of her stomach that life was repeating itself, casting her in the role of nursemaid again. She wanted to turn and run, never stop running.

She heard her name and looked up. Her father was speaking. "You should have seen Maria, Mama. She was so devoted to Rosy. This last year she gave up school, her friends, everything to stay by her mother's side."

Maria turned away, struggling to shut out her father's words. She wanted to cry, *What else could I do, Papa? You were gone all the time. Who else did Mama have?*

Maria pushed her silent accusations to the back of her mind. She hated feeling angry with her father, loving him as she did.

Grandmother Estrella sliced through Maria's thoughts with a lilting, "Come, Maria, we talk of happy things now. I will show you how to make tortillas the way my grandmother made them. *Muy delicioso!*"

The next two days passed all too quickly for Maria. Suddenly her father was packing, saying good-bye, striding with his valise out to his automobile. Maria dreaded seeing him go.

"I'll put up new screens on my next visit," he assured his mother as he stooped to kiss her wreath of gray hair.

He hugged Maria so tightly she could scarcely catch her breath. Then, just as swiftly, he released her and slipped into his car. He closed the door, rolled down the window, and squinted up at her. "I love you, baby."

"Me too, Papa," she said over the lump in her throat.

"Take care of yourself—and Grandma too." His face

clouded. "She's failed so much since I saw her last. Keep an eye on her, OK?"

"I'll try to help her, Papa."

"Good girl. I think she needs you more than you need her."

"You will come back soon, won't you, Papa?"

"I'll do my best, honey. Write me."

"I will." Maria waved vigorously as the familiar, timeworn Plymouth backed out of the driveway. She shouted good-bye, struggling to smile through her tears. But inside she felt as if she were being deserted by the only person she really loved.

3

Maria stood outside the door of Garcia's Grocery, staring at the sign on the weather-beaten door. *Abierto*—Open. She felt repelled by the faded stucco building and its cramped, cluttered windows. Crudely printed signs proclaimed: *pescados, huevos, carne de vaca, frutas y legumbres*. Could anyone inside speak English, or would they expect Maria to know Spanish?

Tentatively she opened the door and slipped inside. A bell jangled noisily, announcing her arrival to all around. Maria stole between two narrow, crowded aisles stacked high with cereal boxes and canned goods. Her eyes roved over the limited merchandise.

A stocky man in a butcher's apron stood behind a counter chatting in Spanish with a stooped, shawled woman. Spotting Maria, the man smiled and called, *"Buenas dias!"*

Maria merely nodded. If she replied in Spanish, the man would assume she knew the language. He spoke again anyway, his inflection suggesting a question. But Maria heard only a barrage of unintelligible sounds. She pivoted and walked out of the store without looking back.

Safeway, here I come! she decided, even though the supermarket was several blocks away. She felt uneasy walking alone through this strange, drab neighborhood. She remembered her grandmother's warnings about gang fights. Would someone snatch her purse or even attack her?

Just before she reached the Safeway store, Maria passed a nondescript brick building with small, bottle-glass windows. The neon sign overhead flashed, "Palermo's Bar and Grill." Two tall, muscular youths with mops of unruly black hair slouched against the structure, smoking. Maria's heartbeat quickened nervously as she felt the strangers' contemptuously appraising glances.

"Hey, *muchacha,* you lost?" sneered the older fellow. He had a long, thin face, thick mustache, and slanting brows. A cigarette bobbed from the left corner of his mouth where a pale, jagged scar jutted from his lower lip to his square chin. He stepped in front of Maria. "If you're lost, babe, I found you."

Maria tried to walk around him. He blocked her way. "Where you going, fine lady?" he persisted. "Maybe I'm going there too."

"Let me by," Maria said, trying to sound in control.

"You new around here? I know all the chicks, but I ain't seen you before."

"Please, I'm in a hurry—"

He placed a restraining hand on her shoulder. "What's your name, pretty lady?"

Maria drew back, trembling. "I don't have time to talk now," she said, breathless with terror.

"Oh, yeah? Well, you got time to talk to Raul—"

"Leave her alone, Raul!" The other youth stepped between them. He was younger and more attractive than his friend, with sultry, penetrating eyes, a straight nose, full, sensual lips, and a gold earring in his right ear. He stared down his comrade. "I said, let her go."

"Stay out of this, Enrique."

"Man, can't you see she's scared?"

Raul released her with a menacing sneer. "We'll talk again, pretty lady—when it's just the two of us."

Maria hurried past him and ran into the Safeway store. Once inside, she found a counter to lean against. Her legs felt wobbly. Her heart pounded like a hammer against tissue paper. There was no way she could carry a bundle of groceries home today. She would have to ask if she could borrow a shopping cart. It would mean two more trips over these ominous streets, but what else could she do? She would have to shop quickly to make the trip back with the cart before dark.

That evening, after her grandmother had gone to bed, Maria sank wearily onto the sofa and propped up her feet. She hoped the groceries would last long enough for her to recover from today's unnerving excursion before venturing out again.

Maria had just begun to doze when she heard a knock at the door. She sprang up apprehensively, her nerves still on edge from her earlier encounter with the two ruffians. She opened the door a crack, keeping the chain lock in place. A deep voice said, "Is Mrs. Estrella home?"

Maria looked up into a frighteningly familiar face with dark, disarming eyes. She gasped. It was the younger of the two youths who had bothered her today. How did he find her? Did he follow her home? Had he come to harm her? Maria was about to slam the door, but something in the young man's expression made her hesitate. He seemed as surprised to see her as she was to see him.

"What do you want?"

"I—I came to see Mrs. Estrella. Is she OK?"

"She's fine. Now go away."

"Wait." The youth put his hand in the door. "You're the girl Raul picked on today."

"What of it?"

"I'm sorry he scared you. He didn't mean no harm."

"If that was your idea of fun—" she began.

"No, it wasn't," he shot back. "I was the one who rescued you, remember?"

"Is that what you call it?"

"Come on, don't be mad at me. I was on your side."

"I don't need you to defend me, whoever you are. Just see that your friend keeps his distance, OK?" Maria attempted to shut the door, but the youth jammed his hand farther inside and demanded, "Wait, I'm not finished."

"What is it now?" she cried in exasperation.

"I want to talk to Mrs. Estrella. She's not sick, is she?"

"How do you know my grandmother?" Maria asked accusingly.

His face registered astonishment. "She's your grandmother?"

"Yes. And, no, she's not sick."

The young man pressed his face against the open space in the doorway. "That's good." He sighed. "When I didn't hear from her, I began to wonder . . ."

Maria frowned, confused. "Why would *you* hear from my grandmother?"

He gazed at her through the narrow space with dark, soulful eyes. "We could talk better if you'd unhook the chain."

"Tell me first how you know my grandmother."

"I do her shopping sometimes. She can't get out so she gives me money and I go buy the stuff she needs."

Maria gaped in surprise. "You're—?"

"Enrique." He smiled. "Enrique Fernandez, at your service."

"I'm sorry," Maria stammered. "I didn't realize you were the neighbor boy my grandmother mentioned. I—I'm glad she had someone to help with her shopping."

"Yeah, well, your grandma's an OK lady. She treats me like somebody, you know?" He reached around and jiggled the chain lock. "So now will you open the door?"

Maria stepped back uncertainly, then shook her head. "No, Mr. Fernandez, go away. Please go away. My grandmother doesn't need your assistance anymore. She has me to shop for her now. If you want to help, just see that your rude friend leaves me alone."

4

It was morning already. The late July sun streamed through the window, urging Maria awake. Before she even opened her eyes or the cobwebs of slumber ebbed away, Maria imagined that she was still back home in Colorado. She could almost hear her mother calling her name. *Maria! Come on, sleepy head. You'll be late for school. Your oatmeal and toast will be cold. Hurry up, sweetheart!*

Maria could practically taste her mother's delicious oatmeal sprinkled with brown sugar, and steaming hot. In these rare moments between dreamy sleep and wakefulness, she could imagine herself sitting at the breakfast table with her mom and dad, everything normal and wonderful and right, the way she used to think it would be forever. She could picture the sunny kitchen, the wallpaper with its pastel roses, the oak table brimming with flowers from her mother's garden. She could see it all—her life as it had been, a life she had taken for granted because she didn't know how quickly it would end.

She could see her father in his best suit, gulping down his coffee and grabbing his briefcase, throwing Maria and her mother kisses as he rushed out the door. He was always in a hurry, always on the move. But Maria and her mother smiled and took it in stride. They savored their leisurely moments alone to catch up on girl talk—wonderful hours filled with dreaming and reminiscing.

Maria could tell her mother anything. They were soul-mates. Her mother always understood, always seemed to know what Maria was feeling before she even expressed what was on her heart.

Some of the girls at school complained that their mothers were mean and demanding and overly strict. But not Maria. She considered her mother her best friend. Even now she knew she would never feel as close to anyone as she had felt to her mother.

Now, to Maria's dismay, there was no one on earth who knew her well—her hopes and dreams and deepest longings; there was no one who considered her special. Oh, of course, there were Dad and Grandma Estrella, but they only knew the surface Maria—the polite, proper, artificial face she presented to the world. They didn't know how to read the inner face of her heart.

Since her mother's death, Maria was never quite sure whether she grieved more for her mother or for herself. Was this intense ache she felt because her mother had died or because Maria had lost her mother's love? Sometimes she felt guilty when she tried to analyze her pain. She didn't want her mourning to be selfish, tied to her own losses. She wanted it to be pure and self-less and focused only on her mother, the beautiful, pure-hearted Rosy Estrella.

But on this warm July morning, as the sun streamed through the windows of Grandma Estrella's little house, Maria despaired that the memories of her mother were slipping away all too quickly. With wakefulness came reality. Maria wasn't still in her cheerful kitchen in Colorado eating oatmeal with brown sugar. She wasn't sitting at the oak table with her mom and dad. And when she tried to hold onto the image of her mother's lovely, smiling face, the memory evaporated like morning mist in sear-ing sunlight.

Maria sat up in bed and rocked back and forth, hugging her arms against her chest. She closed her eyes, willing her mind to re-create her mother's features. But all that came to her was the haunting specter of her mother's pale, haggard face ravaged by cancer.

Maria pushed the bitter memory away and climbed out of bed. She washed and dressed automatically and ran a brush through her long, thick hair. Then she went to the kitchen where Grandma Estrella was already bustling about, making tortillas. "Good morning," said Maria, sitting down.

Grandma Estrella's face lit up. *"Bueno, niña.* Are you hungry?"

Maria shrugged. "Do we have any oatmeal?"

"No, only tortillas, but you go buy at Safeway, no?"

"Sure, Grandmother. I'll go to the Safeway." Maria poured herself a glass of orange juice. "And I'll buy whatever else we need too."

"Is long walk to Safeway. You too tired to carry groceries?"

"No, Grandmother, I don't mind. I've got nothing else to do." It was true, Maria thought ruefully. She had no friends, no place to go. Walking to the Safeway store was the big event of Maria's week.

After breakfast, Maria took paper and pencil and made a list. Milk, Frosted Flakes, tomatoes, detergent, hamburger . . .

"Don't forget onions and garlic," said her grandmother.

Maria nodded. "And bread and butter . . . "

Grandma Estrella reached over and clasped Maria's shoulder. *"Niña,* buy something special for you. Sweets. Something good."

"I don't need anything special, Grandmother."

"Sí. Something to bring happy smile to your sad face."

Maria looked away, suddenly self-conscious. She didn't want her grandmother to see her sadness. She didn't want to seem like an ungrateful child to the one loving person who had taken her in.

"Do you think I do not know?" Grandma Estrella cupped Maria's face in her thick, brown hands. *"Niña mia,* I have torn place in my heart too. Your mama—she was like my child. I love her like I love my Jose."

"Oh, Grandmother!" Maria threw her arms around the elderly woman and held her tight for a long moment. Her voice broke with rising emotion. "I'm sorry. I know you loved my mother too."

Later that morning, as Maria walked to the store, she reflected that she felt a little better after sharing her grief with her grandmother. It was as if there was a new bond between them—their love for Rosy Estrella and their grief in losing her.

That special feeling of closeness lingered as Maria pushed her shopping cart up one aisle and down another. She scanned the shelves—a sea of colorful cartons, cans, and containers. After choosing the items she needed, Maria headed for the checkout counters.

She chose the line with the grocery checker who was always friendly—a blonde, freckled, clean-scrubbed girl who greeted people as if she really cared about them. She had crinkly, laughing eyes and a rangy, boyish frame that matched her casual dress. Her lack of makeup gave her a down-to-earth quality that Maria found refreshing. The girl obviously wasn't hung up with ego or image problems. Her name was Sarah. Sarah Wilms. The name was on her badge. Maria had made a point to remember it.

"Hi, Sarah," Maria greeted as she placed her purchases on the counter.

"Hello—uh, Maria, isn't it?" said Sarah.

"Right. You remembered."

"You're the girl from Colorado. You shop for your grandmother."

"Wow, you really do have a good memory."

Sarah smiled. "I think it's neat you look after your grandmother—do her shopping and all."

"Well, I don't have much else to do until school starts."

Sarah nodded. "I guess it's not so easy making new friends in the summer."

"Especially since I'm from out of state," said Maria.

"Oh, almost everyone in California is from out of state." Sarah laughed as she rang up the total on her register. "That'll be thirty-five eighty-six."

Maria carefully counted out the cash.

"Say, I have an idea," said Sarah. "There's a concert at my church next Sunday. Would you like to go?"

Maria shook her head. "I can't. I don't have a car."

"Oh, well, let me think. I know. I'm catching a ride with this guy from my youth group. We could swing by your way if you tell me where you live."

"No, I—I really couldn't do that."

"Why not? We'd love to have you come with us."

"Well, I—" Maria realized that the other people in line were waiting for her to move on. "Thanks anyway, Sarah," she said quickly, pushing her shopping cart out of the way.

Sarah scrawled something on a slip of paper. "Here's my phone number, Maria. Call me if you change your mind."

Maria nodded and hurried out of store with her groceries. Her face felt flushed with a mixture of excitement and embarrassment. She realized that she had just made her first friend in California. Oh, if only she could attend the concert! Would her grandmother mind? Did Maria dare allow Sarah and this boy she didn't know to pick her up? She didn't want to impose on anybody, and yet Sarah had sounded so genuinely friendly. *We'd love to have you come with us*.

By the time Maria arrived home, she had made her decision. She telephoned Sarah that evening and told her she could go. She counted the days until Sunday, then spent the entire afternoon fretting over what to wear and laboring over her hair and makeup.

For more than half an hour before her ride was due, Maria stood on the front porch, waiting and watching. Then, when a silver-blue Mustang pulled up at the curb, Maria's mouth went dry and her pulse raced. "I'm leaving now, Grandmother," she called as she straightened her shoulders and walked briskly toward the automobile.

Sarah opened the passenger door and leaned forward so Maria could climb in the back seat. "Maria, this is Brett Burkhard," said Sarah. "Brett, Maria."

"Hi, Maria," said Brett with a nod as he shifted into drive. He wore glasses that gave him a wise, owlish look. He wasn't exactly handsome, but he had a certain eccentric, professorial quality. He looked like he could be a scientist, or an elder statesman, or a chess whiz. "Glad you could join us," he said in a voice that was studiously articulate.

"I'm glad you invited me," said Maria politely.

"We should have a great turnout for the concert," Brett continued. "We've been rounding everyone up from the highways and byways."

"What?" asked Maria.

"Oh, that's just a saying, like 'bringing in the sheaves.'"

"I'm sorry, Brett." Maria shrugged helplessly. "Is that California talk?"

Sarah laughed. "No, Maria, it's just 'Christianese.'"

Maria still didn't understand, but she figured it was best not to pursue it. She settled back and drew in a deep breath.

It was a short drive to Amarillo Street. Only two miles to the stately, old-fashioned church with its white spires and quaint belfry. "Oh, it's beautiful," cried Maria. The sign in front read "Community Bible Church." Over the door hung a banner proclaiming, "Contemporary Christian Concert. Everyone Welcome."

The building was packed with laughing, shouting teenagers, and the air bristled with excitement and anticipation. "Come on, Maria," Sarah called over the din. "Our group has a section of seats reserved near the front."

Maria followed Sarah and Brett down the aisle, but there were only two seats left. "Sit right behind us, Maria," said Sarah.

Maria looked tentatively at the empty seat beside a strapping redheaded boy. "Excuse me," she said shyly, "is that seat saved?"

"Naw," the boy guffawed, "it ain't even under conviction!"

Maria wasn't sure whether that meant the seat was free or not, but she decided to chance it and sit down. The redhead frowned and muttered something to his buddy about girls who couldn't take a joke. His buddy, a blond boy with a lightning grin that stole Maria's breath—and heart—smiled at her and said, "Hi. I'm Lonnie. You ever hear the Gospel Warriors?"

"No," said Maria, flustered, reeling from the boy's magnetic gaze. "Are—are they good?"

"Dynamite. Almost as good as the Radical Rocking Saints. You'll love them."

The lights dimmed then, saving Maria from the embarrassment of admitting she had never heard of either musical group. But even in the dark she could still see the blond boy's infectious smile. She knew already she would never forget it. Or *him*. He said his name was Lonnie. Lonnie what?

The audience began to clap loudly as a trio of male performers in acid-wash Levi's and jean jackets sprinted onto the stage amid flashing lights and a surging drum roll. One youth took the keyboard, another picked up a guitar, and the third grabbed the microphone and began to sing. Maria expected the typical rock sound, but this group had a mixture of soul and pop, with a touch of country. But what Maria noticed most were their words. Every song was about Jesus.

Jesus is the answer/He can heal all your pain/fill your heart with gladness/turn your losses into gain.

Jesus is the answer/He died hanging on a tree/came alive to reign in heaven/He welcomes you and me.

One joyous, exhilarating song led to another, and another. Maria was caught up in the energy of the pulsating rhythms and thrilled by the upbeat lyrics. She felt surprisingly alive, or on the verge of being really alive. What was it? She couldn't quite grasp what it was about—these young people and their lilting, rollicking songs about Jesus.

Before the final number, one singer took the microphone and said, "Friends, what it comes down to for every one of us on this earth is that we're looking for love. Unconditional love. We want someone to love us just as we are, faults and all. Well, I'm here to tell you, Someone does. His name is Jesus, and when you've felt His love in your heart, you know what real love is all about. And what this life is all about. That's why I sing love songs about Jesus. Is His love song playing in your heart?"

Maria mulled over the question. Was Jesus' love song playing in her heart? Not likely. As far as she knew, no song played in her heart. But what a wonderful thought—a love song playing forever in her heart!

But then, all too quickly, before anyone even explained how she could get that special song, the evening was over. The shouts and applause resounded in Maria's ears as the crowd surged out of the auditorium. Maria looked around for one more glimpse of the boy named Lonnie, but he was already walking out with an attractive girl with long, strawberry-blonde tresses.

Wordlessly Maria followed Sarah and Brett to his car and climbed in. She felt a sinking sensation as the silver-blue Mustang sped her back to her dingy neighborhood. She had been touched by so many special things tonight—the music, the young people, the idea of Jesus being her Friend. But with the mystery of His love unsolved and Jesus still beyond her reach, Maria found herself back in the old, familiar barrio in the dreary deadness of summer.

In the days that followed, Maria's special evening at the concert became like a dream. Elusive. Unreal. Sadly, she wondered, was her mind playing tricks? Maybe it never occurred. Maybe it meant nothing at all.

5

Summer was passing with a dreadful tedium. Mentally Maria marked off the last days of July on Grandma Estrella's wall calendar. It was finally August—a sun-drenched Wednesday afternoon—as if the day or month made any difference! Life was the same dreary routine, no matter how time was divided or tagged.

Today was unusually hot, humid, and sticky for California weather. Maria didn't want to do anything but sit and sip iced tea and be thankful for the rare breeze skittishly bombarding the windows.

Nearly all the windows of the house were open. There was just the fine blackened barrier of screens to keep the compact rooms from being vulnerable to hordes of flies buzzing against the protective netting. Maria could see the insects' quick, wiry black legs poking through and prodding the small, neat spaces of the screen, trying to invade the premises somehow.

The screens were old, crude. Her father should have replaced them when he was here. There were lots of small gaping holes like wounds through which the bugs would sneak inside and then, at night, buzz the ceiling light exultantly, triumphant. When the breeze died down, the house was hot in spite of all the open windows, so Maria fled outside and sank with relief onto the scratchy, broken porch steps. But even here everything stood still—the grass, the trees, even Maria's clothes on the line—as if the whole world were waiting, wilted and without energy, for August to be over. It irritated Maria that life at Grandma Estrella's seemed to be an endless matter of keeping cool and quenching thirst and swatting flies.

She sat back against the rough-hewn porch and reflected that the only exciting event since her arrival was last Sunday's contemporary Christian concert at the Community Bible Church two miles from her neighborhood. What an evening it had turned out to be. What fun! What excitement! Maria had glimpsed a promise of hope and joy: the incredible idea of Jesus being her personal Friend. The thrill of belonging, of being part of the young people's group. But all too soon she had been whisked back home again, back to her old, oppressive neighborhood. How she wished she could go back and relive that evening again!

Incredibly, even while Maria sat on the porch now fanning herself, the memory of the concert was brought back fresh again just as a shiny red Chevrolet pulled up before Grandma Estrella's house. Maria recognized Sarah Wilms, Lonnie with the lightning grin, and three other young people from the church. Eagerly, with broad smiles and bright, intense eyes, they bounded from the automobile and swarmed onto the porch. Maria stood up and looked from one to the other and back again, smiling foolishly, hugging her arms against her chest. "Sarah, I'm so surprised—" she began.

A tall, tanned young man introduced himself as Michael Dodd, the youth director from Community Bible Church. He carried a large Bible, a stack of little white cards, and some magazine-sized pamphlets under his arm. "Our youth group is calling on those who came to the concert last Sunday night," he explained. "We want you to know how happy we were to have you with us."

"I had a good time, I really did," Maria said, pushing back her long dark hair that clung like damp tentacles to her warm neck.

"Well," said Sarah, beaming, "we just want you to know you're welcome at our church anytime."

"Any time," echoed a girl whose name Maria didn't know.

"Well, won't you come in?" asked Maria eagerly. "Won't you stay a while and meet my grandmother? We could have some sun tea and talk a little."

Michael looked mildly doubtful. "I don't know. Maybe we could stay just a minute."

"We have a lot of other names to call on yet," Sarah explained kindly, pointing to the cards in Michael's hand. "We had over twenty new kids in our church last Sunday, can you imagine?"

"Over twenty," echoed someone significantly.

Maria brushed unconsciously at the fine mist of perspiration on her forehead. "Well, it's so warm, I thought maybe a quick glass of sun tea . . . My grandmother keeps it made in the icebox."

Michael seemed to brighten a little. "Well, sure, I guess we can stay a minute. We can stay that long anyway."

The kids followed Maria into the house and settled onto the couch or into chairs while she went to the kitchen for glasses of iced tea. She was serving the tea when her grandmother entered with her elderly neighbor, Mrs. Ramiriz. The two women were absorbed in conversation, both speaking at once in their rapid, spirited Spanish. When Grandma Estrella spotted Maria's guests, she stopped in mid-sentence and broke into a surprised smile.

"I have guests, Grandmother," Maria said quickly. "From the church I attended last Sunday."

Grandma Estrella said something briefly to her neighbor, gesturing toward the young people. Maria winced. How she wished her grandmother would speak English! Then her grandmother turned to the visitors and opened her arms expansively. "I welcome friends of Maria. I am happy to have you here."

Maria flushed slightly and a few drops of tea sloshed over the rims of the glasses she held out to her guests. She stumbled self-consciously through introductions, while the young people turned on thin, brief smiles and murmured appropriately, "Hello, Mrs. Estrella, Mrs. Ramiriz. How are you . . . glad to know you."

"We were just telling Maria how happy we were to have her attend our concert last Sunday," said Sarah pleasantly.

Grandma Estrella nodded vaguely. "Maria enjoy the church. She like the—the friends." She hesitated, then apologized. "Excuse me. My English . . . is not so good."

"Well, we'd be happy to have Maria back any time," said the boy named Lonnie, smiling that smile of his.

"I would love to come if I had a way," said Maria in a soft, eager voice. "But, you see, we have no car."

"Well, come when you can," replied a pretty girl named Lauren.

"Yes," agreed Michael. "Now we really must be going."

"I hoped we could talk a little," said Maria tentatively.

"Is there something special you wanted to talk about?" asked Sarah.

Maria shrugged, biting her lip thoughtfully. "I was curious about the songs at the concert—the words, what they said about Jesus."

Sarah smiled. "I'm glad you want to know, Maria."

"We have these booklets," said Michael, handing her one of the large pamphlets he carried. "This will explain just what we believe."

"Michael, we really should be going," Lauren whispered. "The other names . . . "

"I want to hear all about what you believe," said Maria, clasping the booklet to her chest. "I want to . . . "

Lonnie smiled, but there was no lightning in his grin this time. "We do have these other names to call on," he said lamely. "It was nice meeting you ladies, but, well, we'd better go."

Maria looked at him. "Yes, yes, of course," she agreed at once, squelching the disappointment, a kind of hurt, rising in her throat.

"Please do come to our church anytime you can, Maria," called Sarah as the group filed evenly out the door and was absorbed into the waiting automobile.

"Anytime!" someone shouted over the roar of the engine.

After the red Chevrolet had pulled away, Maria went inside and wandered through the house, clearing away tea glasses and partly lowering the windows against the approaching night. Later, after Mrs. Ramiriz had left and Grandmother Estrella had gone to bed, Maria turned on the overhead light in the living room and sat down to read the pamphlet Michael had given her. It was growing dark now, and a breeze was stirring, quite cool for a change, blowing out the bottom parts of the curtains, turning them into great sacks of air. The breeze made the pages flutter a little, and the words seemed hard to read somehow, as if they were not real, as if they were part of a dream that might never quite be grasped.

Then, suddenly, Maria was aware of an insistent, irritating hum—the buzzing of flies around the overhead light. She watched them curiously for a moment and then went to the kitchen for the fly swatter. It wasn't in its place hanging from the nail by the back door. Where had Grandma Estrella left it?

On impulse, Maria rolled up the pamphlet Michael had given her and returned to the living room. She had to stand on a chair to reach the pesky insects, but it was well worth the slight dizziness she felt on looking down. Carefully she aimed her weapon and swatted, and one by one the flies fell. She saw them scattered about on the floor, crumpled up, curled crazily, dead as doornails. *They got theirs,* she thought triumphantly. No more disturbing hum, no nasty buzzing. She took care of them, all right.

When she had finished, she stepped off the chair, aware of a peculiar sense of satisfaction gradually distilling the yawning emptiness—that strange sense of loss she had felt earlier watching the red Chevrolet pull away from the house. She was fine now, she told herself. Fine.

With perfect efficiency, she scooped the flies up with the pamphlet and dumped everything into the trash. With a quick, deliberate gait, she returned to the living room and settled once again into her chair. But for some reason she could not think of what to do now, nor of what she had been about to do. She stared at her hands, which appeared almost sallow under the harsh glare of the overhead light. Only then, holding her hands out empty beneath the light, did she notice that the entire house seemed to swell with an absolute, deadening silence. It was strange, she thought. Crazy. Like the emptiness easing back into her bones, it made no sense.

6

As the same, sultry days of August wore on, Maria decided, almost in desperation, to visit Community Bible Church again. As she saw it, the teenagers she had met there offered the only potential for fun and companionship in an otherwise bleak existence. For the next three Sundays Maria took the city bus to the large stucco church on Amarillo Street.

She raised her hand her first time in Sunday school when the teacher asked for visitors to identify themselves. Afterward, two girls paused to say they were glad to have her there, and the lightning-grin boy named Lonnie smiled as he passed by. In the church service, Maria sat with Sarah Wilms, her friend from the Safeway store.

The next Sunday Maria was no longer a first-time visitor, so she didn't raise her hand. This time no one stopped to speak, although two girls nodded hello. Maria looked around for Sarah, then remembered that she would be on vacation with her family for the rest of August. The others who had called on her were nowhere in sight. Maria tried not to feel disappointed. She reminded herself she was still a stranger here. It would take time to become acquainted, to be accepted as part of the group.

This morning was Maria's third Sunday at church. During Sunday school she made it a point to smile at anyone who glanced her way. When someone said hello, she quickly offered her name and started a conversation rolling. She felt especially optimistic when she learned there would be a get-together at the youth leader's home after the evening service.

"Everyone's invited, so you all be sure and come," said the handsome Lonnie making the announcements.

Everyone's invited, thought Maria. *That means me too. At last I'll have a chance to make some real friends!*

On Sunday afternoon, Maria could scarcely keep down the excitement bubbling inside her. Tonight would be special, she was sure of it. To keep her enthusiasm in check, she spent the afternoon picking out her favorite tunes on Grandma Estrella's old piano. Since coming to California, Maria had spent countless hours at this beloved, untuned piano. She played well by ear, even though she had never taken lessons. At times her fingers seemed touched by magic as they danced over the worn keys.

If only she could read the notes! A dream, of course. Fragile as Grandma Estrella's ceramic Madonna. Dreams were like wishes, like smoke, escaping from the fires of one's heart, spiraling heavenward, only to be buffeted by winds, to fade swiftly into nothing, air.

Playing the piano always made Maria feel reflective. Especially this afternoon. She recalled that in the past two years she had lost many dreams as easily as smoke. Still, in spite of everything, she clung to a stubborn optimism. *Let go of hope, and you let go of everything.* Her mother had said that once during the early days of her illness. Before the ravages of cancer tore through her body devastating her health and strength. During the funeral Maria had forced her mind to remember the warm, vibrant person her mother had been, refusing to admit that the emaciated body in the casket was her mother's.

So there it was. Hope number one had been dashed to the ground. To have a mother. Something as basic and simple as a mother! Hope number two had been that somehow Maria and her father could survive as a family, heal their wounds, and go on to create some sort of life together.

The memory still tore at Maria's heart—her father explaining why he was taking her to Grandma Estrella's to live. It would never be the rosy picture her father had painted. Maria and Grandma Estrella didn't make a family. They were two separate, very different people living under the same roof. Too often Maria felt overwhelmed by an agonizing loneliness—for her mother, for her father, for friends to replace those she had left back home.

Of course, Maria realized her grandmother was trying to reach out, trying to build a bridge between them. Just last week, when Maria had admired the ceramic Madonna on the small buffet, her grandmother said, "You may have her if you like."

"Do you mean it?" Maria had cried, pleased. Since then the lovely Madonna had stood on Maria's dresser, seemingly a promise of good things to come. Thinking of the pure young Mary, mother of Jesus, Maria resolved to be someone her father and grandmother would be proud of, a woman brave and lovely and good, like Mary.

Picturing the Madonna now, Maria's fingers rose and fell liltingly on the smooth ivory keys—rhapsodic music to express the wordless stirrings in her soul. The mood broke as Maria became aware of a rustle of clothing behind her. She turned to see Grandma Estrella in her bathrobe, her wispy gray hair spun in a halo around her head.

"My arthritis is bad, *querida*," she said. "I go to bed early."

"Do you want me to stay home with you?" Maria asked.

"No, *niña*. You go to church. Have good time."

"If you're sure, Grandmother." Maria smiled. "I have a feeling good things are going to happen tonight."

Grandma Estrella nodded. "You deserve good things, Maria." She reached out and affectionately patted Maria's hand. "You are good girl. Now go along, before you miss your bus."

Maria still didn't feel at ease going to church by herself. Tonight, as usual, there was the long, lonely bus ride with strangers ogling her from across the aisle. Then, as she feared, she sat alone during the church service surrounded by couples and threesomes. It seemed that everyone belonged with someone, except Maria.

She didn't relax until the minister began his sermon. Tonight, his words had a special way of drilling into her mind, making her thoughts stand at attention. He talked of things that had always been a mystery to her. The love of God. God's provision for the sins of mankind. The way of salvation through Jesus

Christ. What did these words mean? "Believe on the Lord Jesus Christ and you will be saved," the pastor read from his Bible.

Believe what? Be saved from what? Maria wondered urgently. She clutched the pew in front of her while the congregation sang a hymn in slow, accustomed voices. Maria's thoughts pulled frantically in opposite directions. *Go forward. Find this Jesus. No! Stay where you are.*

Then, surprisingly, the service was over and people were filing out. Maria waited until her heart stopped hammering in her ears. She had not had to make a decision yet. There was still time. Another time!

For now, all Maria wanted to think about was the teen get-together at the youth leader's home. With a fresh thrill of anticipation, she made her way through the crowd, looking for a familiar face. Spotting the attractive strawberry blonde standing with several other young people, Maria made her way over and said hello. When the girl gave her a blank, curious stare, Maria quickly explained, "You called on me last month after the concert, and we talked a minute in Sunday school this morning, remember?"

"Oh, yes," said the girl with a surprised, affected laugh. "It's good to see you again." She tossed her long, loosely styled hair. "I'm Lauren Pettegrew. Are you going to the party?"

Maria's face felt warm, flushed. "Well, yes, I want to go. But I'm not sure how to get there."

"It's at Michael Dodd's, our youth director. Know where he lives?"

Maria shook her head.

"Well, it's on Brentwood—or Baywood." The girl turned to the handsome boy beside her. "Lonnie, what's Michael's street?"

"Baywood," he supplied.

"Hey, Lonnie, did you bring your cassette tapes?" someone asked.

"They're in the car. That new group has a sound you wouldn't believe."

Maria followed the conversation silently, straining to think of something to offer. Several others dropped in and out of the conversation, mingling a moment, then wandering off elsewhere. Glancing around, Maria noticed that the crowd was thinning out. Several of the group had already left. She turned back to Lauren, but the girl was walking off toward the door with Lonnie.

With a sudden swell of anxiety, Maria looked around for another familiar face. She noticed two guys talking animatedly. One looked familiar. He was Brett something, the boy who had driven Sarah and her to the concert last month. The other fellow was saying, "Michael asked me to give devotions tonight. I plan to discuss how our group can reach others for Christ. I have some good theories on reaching the unchurched."

Maria approached hesitantly and asked, "Could you tell me how I could get to Brent—Baywood? To Michael Dodd's house?"

Brett flashed a benevolent smile. "Sure. Go straight down Clinton to Baywood about two miles. You can't miss it."

Maria smiled to cover her embarrassment. "I guess I should explain—"

The other young man interrupted with a grin. "Excuse me, but I must return this book to the pastor. See you later, OK?"

Maria looked helplessly at Brett and, steeling herself, asked, "Are *you* going to the party tonight?"

The wiry, sandy-haired youth chuckled and pushed his glasses up on his nose. "No, not tonight," he sighed. He walked with Maria to the door. "I've got a history report due for summer school. Sorry."

Maria nodded miserably and watched in silence as Brett strode outside. She looked around the vestibule and realized she was practically alone. With an involuntary shiver she went out the door into the brooding darkness. It was too late now to catch the bus, so she walked home alone, sidestepping every shadow, squelching the terror that pulsed icily in her veins. Knowing Grandma Estrella would be asleep, Maria climbed the creaky porch steps on tiptoe and quietly unlocked the door. She slipped into the house and stole to her room.

What had happened tonight? Nothing. Everything.

"How about that?" Maria whispered through her teeth, lightly, so that the sound could not go anywhere. "How about that? Another dream bit the dust. Just like that!"

As Maria undressed for bed, moonlight streamed through the bedroom window illuminating objects with slivers of silver— the dresser, her mother's framed portrait, the little ceramic Madonna Grandma Estrella had given her. For a long moment Maria stared curiously at the fragile figurine. She chewed her lower lip, thinking, mulling things over in her mind. Then, on impulse, she reached out and touched the statue reassuringly with her fingertips. At the moment it was the only real, tangible thing in her life. It felt smooth, solid, almost comforting. As Maria withdrew her hand, she caught a glimpse of unexpected movement. The ceramic figure wobbled momentarily, then toppled off the dresser, shattering noisily.

Maria stared in astonishment at the white shards of glass on the floor. She knelt down in the moon-washed darkness, shaking her head, stunned. Then, carefully, with a tissue she swept the splintered fragments into a pile under her dresser. In the morning she would throw the remnants into the trash. After all, it was only a statue, she argued, swallowing her tears. It couldn't promise good things. It wasn't lucky or magical. It was just a knickknack. Maybe, just maybe, Grandma Estrella wouldn't even notice it was gone.

As Maria stood and gazed from where the statue had been to the shadowed portrait of her mother, sobs rose in a solid mass in her throat. "Why do I always lose everything I love?" she cried in a raw whisper. With tears streaming down her face, she took the framed picture over to the window and studied it in the moonlight. Rosy Estrella couldn't have been more than twenty-five when the photo was taken. It showed her in a ruby-red velvet blouse, her head turned dreamily to one side, her golden-auburn hair flowing luxuriantly down her back. She had large, green, doe-soft eyes and a flawless roses-and-cream complexion.

Maria always wanted to remember her mother as she was in this portrait, not the way she looked during those final days. But one image was inescapable—her mother's dying. Only Maria was there during those last moments to offer comfort and cradle her mother's head in her lap. It was a memory Maria would never forget and for which she would never quite forgive her father.

Maria's tears spilled unchecked onto the portrait. Why was it, she wondered, that every new hurt and disappointment brought her back to this greater pain—the loss of her mother? What did it matter that others were uncaring or that a treasured statue broke? Nothing could change the bitter fact of Maria's aloneness. Nothing could bring back her mother. Nothing could fill the terrible emptiness she felt. Maria threw herself on her bed and wept uncontrollably, muffling her grief in her pillow. Even at her mother's death she hadn't cried this brokenly.

When her tears were spent, Maria rose and padded to the bathroom. She turned the faucet on low so her grandmother wouldn't hear and washed her face, removing the splotches of mascara under her eyes. She felt drained, without energy. Her scrubbed face looked blank, expressionless in the antique mirror. She had the sensation that, perhaps with a little more scrubbing, she would simply disappear.

The idea was rather appealing. If she were dead like her mother or broken like the Madonna, she couldn't feel pain. She wouldn't ever be lonely again. Reflecting on those possibilities, Maria returned to her room, climbed into bed, and pulled the covers up tight around her like a shield, a protective barrier, final and absolute.

7

On the last Monday of August, Maria spotted Sarah Wilms at the Safeway checkout counter. Sarah's blonde, wind-tossed hair and clean-scrubbed face always made Maria feel brighter inside. Waving Maria over, Sarah called, "Hey, how've you been, Maria?"

Maria placed several grocery items on the counter. "I'm OK. How was your vacation?"

"Great," enthused Sarah. "We saw my grandparents in Seattle. But they couldn't handle the shenanigans of my eight-year-old twin brothers, so my folks decided to come back early." She rang up Rice Krispies, a carton of milk, and a dozen eggs. "We got in late Saturday night. I thought I'd never get up in time for church . . . but I did." She bagged Maria's purchases and smiled. "I was hoping to see you in church yesterday, Maria."

Maria handed Sarah a ten-dollar bill. "I went a few times while you were gone, Sarah, but, well, it's not much fun riding the bus." She didn't add that people hadn't been all that friendly either.

Sarah nodded sympathetically. "My parents don't attend church, so I usually catch a ride with Brett Burkhard. He's the one who drove us to the concert, remember? The intellectual guy with thick glasses and kind of a sweet, homely face."

"I remember him," said Maria.

"Maybe he could pick you up sometime, too."

Maria shook her head doubtfully. "He seems pretty busy with summer school and stuff."

Sarah nodded. "He's always into a hundred things at once—one of those scholastic superstars, you know? But he's very nice, and I'm sure he wouldn't mind driving you once in a while."

"I'll think about it," said Maria, picking up her bag of groceries.

"Don't just think about it," replied Sarah. "You be ready Sunday morning. I'll see to it that Brett picks you up."

Sarah was true to her word. At nine on Sunday, Brett pulled up in his silver-blue Mustang. Maria squeezed into the back seat between Sarah's two pint-size brothers—Willie and Wally Wilms. They were exact replicas—stocky, blond, freckled imps with mischievous smiles. They wiggled and squirmed and shot rubber bands across Maria until she decided that perhaps riding the bus wasn't so bad after all. Brett kept up a nonstop conversation with Sarah about the latest software he was buying for his home computer. Sarah chatted about her trip to Seattle, but Maria, caught between the fidgeting youngsters, couldn't concentrate on anything Brett or Sarah said.

After church, Brett stopped at a Taco Bell and treated everyone to burritos and tostadas. They ate in the car. While Sarah's brothers greedily devoured their lunch, Maria tried in vain to protect her new print shirt dress from hot sauce and shredded cheese.

That evening Maria rode the bus to church. When she didn't spot Brett and Sarah in the sanctuary, she sat beside Lonnie and Lauren. They seemed too absorbed in each other to notice Maria. Maria didn't mind. Her attention was focused on the pastor and what he was saying about Jesus. No one else had ever made Jesus seem so real, so loving, so genuinely concerned about people.

Over the years Maria had attended church only sporadically. She had been awestruck by the elaborate rites and rituals, but she couldn't remember hearing about a personal Jesus who loved her enough to die for her. Surely the words had been there somewhere; she recalled the crucifixes showing Jesus hanging on a cross, His body twisted, His eyes full of anguish. Why had she never made the connection between His sacrifice so long ago and His boundless love for her now? Did Jesus really want her to invite Him into her life, as the pastor said? The idea of God Himself waiting for a personal invitation from a near-orphan named Maria Estrella struck her as utterly absurd. Yet, if it were true . . . if God so loved Maria that He gave up His only Son. . . . Maria marveled over the idea as she rode the city bus home from church. She sat in the back of the bus and stared out the window so that strangers wouldn't think she was inviting conversation. But her attempt at aloofness was wasted as three straggly-haired teenagers behind her pushed their knees jarringly against her seat. When she ignored them, they pushed all the harder, talking in loud, swaggering voices, using words that made Maria blush.

At the next stop, Maria moved to the front of the bus. The youths followed, laughing raucously, stepping on her heels. They slid into the seat behind her, whistling and making catcalls.

"Keep it down," the driver bellowed.

The boys jeered back. "What's a pretty girl like you doing out without her mama?" one taunted.

"Where you live, babe?" another pressed.

Finally, Maria whirled around and glared at them. "Stop it! Leave me alone!"

"Wow, the lady has a temper," the boy in a grimy T-shirt hooted.

Maria stared out the window at the passing lights and shadows. Just a few more stops before the bus reached her neighborhood. Did she dare get off alone? Would these hoodlums follow?

At the next stop, a lone man in Levi's and a black muscle shirt boarded and took the seat two rows ahead. Maria sank back in dismay as she recognized Enrique Fernandez. At least he wasn't with that brute Raul, she noted.

Suddenly Maria felt a painful tug on her cascading curls. One youth leaned over the back of her seat and pursed his lips in an ugly, mocking kiss while his comrades laughed derisively.

Enrique spun around and stared back at them, his eyes hard coals. But as his gaze settled on Maria, he broke into a spontaneous grin. He stood abruptly and strode back to her seat. Fixing his gaze on the teenagers, he demanded, "Beat it, geeks. This here is my lady."

The youths sat back sullenly while Enrique settled down beside Maria. She looked over sheepishly. "Thank you."

He nodded. "That's twice."

"Twice?"

"That I've come to your rescue. Of course . . . who's counting?"

Maria smiled warily. She smelled alcohol and cigarettes on Enrique's breath. Was he really her rescuer, or did he just want to save her for himself? "I get off at the next stop," she murmured.

"Me too."

"I forgot. You live on my grandmother's street, don't you?"

"Even if I didn't, I'd see you home. Pretty girls shouldn't be out alone after dark, not around here." He leaned over confidentially. "Our neighborhood's not so bad, but a few blocks over is gang territory. Strangers don't come out of there alive."

"You're kidding. People don't really live that way, not here in America."

"You don't know nothing about it." He pointed out the window. "You see all the writing on them walls?"

Maria squinted into the darkness. "I've seen the graffiti before. It shows real disrespect for property."

Enrique hooted. "Says you! Man, it's our way of saying who we are. That stuff comes straight from the heart." He grinned. "When I got my can of spray paint going, I feel special, like a real artist, you know?"

"You mean all those words and pictures scrawled everywhere actually mean something?"

"They mean plenty," Enrique declared. "They tell which gangs are at war. They tell whose territory it is. And they warn stay out where you don't belong. If a gang messes up another gang's wall, they're dead."

"Are you saying you're a gang member, Enrique?"

"I don't run with no gang, but everyone's gotta line up with one—you know, be loyal, if you don't want no trouble."

The huge vehicle stopped with a shuddering screech. Enrique helped Maria down from the bus, but she shook his hand from her elbow as soon as her feet touched the ground. The three young ruffians also exited. Maria stole a backward glance, satisfying herself that they were going in the opposite direction. In spite of herself, she felt relieved to have Enrique walking beside her in his long, smooth stride.

"By the way, where were you tonight?" he asked.

"Church."

"Really? My mama used to go a long time ago."

"She doesn't anymore?"

"Nah. She's too busy. She cleans bathrooms in hotels. When she's home, the little ones keep her running."

"Your brothers and sisters?"

"My brothers. I got four. And one sister."

"It must be nice being part of a large family," she mused.

"My old man don't think so. Most of the time he can't find jobs. Rest of the time he's too drunk to work. I don't see him much."

"I'm sorry. It must be very hard for your mother."

"I take care of her," Enrique said proudly. "I work when I can."

"What do you do?"

"Construction jobs for my uncle. In Paramount. Off and on. That's where I was today. See?" He held out scarred, calloused hands under the street light. "No one in my family starves. I see to that."

"I hope you don't have all the responsibility yourself."

Enrique gave her a sidelong glance. "I got one older brother in the army, another in jail, and my sister's pregnant. My two younger brothers are too little to help out. So that leaves me."

"How did you ever have time to shop for my grandmother?"

"I managed. She paid me. Besides, I liked her."

"She likes you too."

"How about you, Maria? You got family—besides your grandma?"

Maria winced. She was growing breathless trying to match Enrique's easy stride. "My mom's dead," she said at last. "My dad's . . . away on business."

Enrique gave her a knowing grimace. "I know how that goes—a permanent trip, right?"

Maria bristled. "Not at all. My dad will be back for me soon, just you wait and see."

"You're the one who'll be waiting," Enrique predicted. They lapsed into silence for several moments. Then, as they approached a Little Italy Pizzeria, he asked, "Are you hungry?"

"No," Maria lied. She glanced through the tinted windows of the quaint little restaurant. There were intimate tables and booths, a video arcade, and a large-screen TV over the bar. She inhaled the hot spicy aromas of sausage, onions, and green peppers. Pizza sounded wonderful, but not tonight; not with Enrique Fernandez. He was still an unknown quantity, a big question mark. He seemed nice enough; yet there was something volatile and unpredictable about him. He could be dangerous; he could be playing a game with her, biding his time until he was ready to strike.

"Maybe some other time?" he said. "You know, go out for pizza?"

Maria shrugged. The air was growing chilly. There was just half a block more to her grandmother's house. Suddenly the dingy little house looked very inviting. "You mean . . . a date?" she asked doubtfully.

"Sure, a date. Why not?"

"I don't know, Enrique. We'll see, OK?"

8

On the second Monday in September, Maria started high school. She faced the first day of her junior year with a mixture of anticipation and excitement. At last she was escaping the doldrums of summer. She would be attending classes, taking part in extra-curricular activities, and—most important—making friends.

When she tried out for student choir, Mr. Jensen told her, "You have one of the best soprano voices I've heard in several years. I'd like you to sign up for Women's Ensemble. And talk to Lonnie Sandstrom over there. He's our best tenor. Leads Madrigal Singers. Perhaps he can work you into his group too."

Maria followed Mr. Jensen's gaze over to the handsome young man with the sturdy, heart-shaped face, determined jaw, and blond, wavy hair. It was Lonnie of the lightning grin. Lauren's Lonnie. The most popular boy at church. He had smiled vaguely at her when she entered the classroom, but did he even remember who she was?

Mr. Jensen beckoned to Lonnie and explained his plans for Maria. "This gal could be a real asset to Madrigal Singers," he suggested.

"I heard her," said Lonnie. "She sounded great." His deep, sable-brown eyes met hers and lingered. Maria sensed with a sudden thrill that he was seeing her for the very first time. "It means a lot of long hours and hard work," he said, his gaze so penetrating she felt flustered, confused.

"I—I'm not afraid of work," she mumbled.

"Good." His smile struck a warm response deep inside her. A loud buzzer sounded, signaling the end of fourth period. Maria turned to gather her books, but Lonnie caught her arm and said, "I'll walk you to lunch. It'll give us a chance to talk."

As they walked to the cafeteria, Lonnie's six-foot frame towered above her. His lean, muscular arm brushed hers casually as they dodged the oncoming streams of students spilling out of classrooms.

"I've seen you around church," Lonnie remarked. "You been attending long?"

"Off and on all summer," said Maria.

He looked at her. "Really? How'd you happen to come?"

"Sarah Wilms invited me." Maria paused, then gave Lonnie a sidelong glance. "You called on me in July, remember?"

Lonnie frowned, then scratched his head, embarrassed. "Of course! You're the girl with the little Spanish grandmother."

Maria nodded. That really wasn't how she wanted him to think of her—as someone different, foreign.

"What about your folks?" he asked.

"They're dead." She hadn't meant to include her father in that statement, but there it was—words spoken that couldn't be snatched back. In a sense, her father *was* dead. He had rejected her. But Lonnie must never know that. What would he think of her? *There's a girl whose own father didn't want her. What a loser!*

"That must be rough," Lonnie was saying.

"What?"

"Losing both your parents. That's a real bummer."

They were in the tray line now, gathering silverware and napkins. She selected a small dish of fresh fruit. "I'm looking forward to singing in the school chorus," she said, switching to a safer topic.

Lonnie reached for a large chef's salad. "Have you had professional training, Maria?"

"Not exactly. I was in girls' chorus and the school choir back in Colorado."

"Well, their loss is our gain," he quipped, bathing her in that smile of his. "You can tell me all about your musical back-

45

ground during lunch." As Lonnie selected a cheeseburger and two small cartons of milk, Maria reached for a plate of macaroni and cheese. They each paid the cashier, then Lonnie said, "Follow me, Maria."

Was it possible that Lonnie Sandstrom actually wanted to spend his lunch hour just with her? Maria followed him through the maze of crowded tables to a far corner of the cafeteria where the wall was decorated with silver-framed sports award plaques. As she glanced from the wall to the table, Maria's eyes settled on a disturbingly familiar face: Lauren Pettegrew's.

Lonnie set his tray on the table and handed Lauren the chef's salad and milk. "Lauren, you know Maria . . . from church?" he said. "She's joining us for lunch."

Lauren brushed back her long hair and appraised Maria with skeptical, ice-blue eyes. A touch of pink blush accented her high cheekbones. "Maria? Why, yes. I remember. You're new here, aren't you?"

Maria felt repelled by Lauren's throaty, bored tone. She forced herself to reply, "I've been here in California for a couple of months."

Lauren's precise red lips settled into a pout. "I should remember, but I'm awful with last names, Maria, especially foreign ones—"

"It's Estrella," said Maria quickly, sitting down.

"What country are you from?" asked Lauren, delicately spearing a tomato wedge from her salad.

"Colorado," said Maria thickly.

"Oh, I mean before that," Lauren tittered.

Maria lifted her chin with proud defiance. "My father's family came from Mexico and Colombia. My mother was Irish."

"Well, my father is Swedish and my mother French," announced Lonnie, affecting each accent with mock exaggeration. "And, Lauren, as I recall, you're rather a mixed bag too—a little French, a bit of English, some German—"

Lauren arched her feathery brows and snapped, "Your lunch is getting cold, Lonnie."

They ate in silence for several minutes. Then Lonnie said, "You should hear Maria sing, Lauren. She's incredible." He

46

looked at Maria. "I won't let you rest until you join the church choir."

Lauren eyed Maria coldly. "Are you a church member, Maria?"

"No, I'm not."

Lonnie looked over curiously. "Have you considered joining?"

Maria shifted uncomfortably. "I don't know." How could she explain to Lonnie that she felt like an outsider in his church? She wasn't even sure what the pastor meant when he talked about being "born again."

"She probably already has her own church, Lonnie," said Lauren.

"No, I don't," Maria corrected. "But my grandmother is a very religious woman. And I want—" What did she want? The words wouldn't come. For weeks Maria had felt the tug of something on her heart. Or was it Someone? At times she sincerely wanted to give her life to Jesus, but how was it supposed to happen? Was it simply a matter of joining a church, saying prayers, attending services? "I want to join a church someday," she said at last, "when I understand things better."

"Well, I hope you pick *my* church," said Lonnie meaningfully. His smile was all Maria's.

That afternoon, as Maria walked home from school, her feet nearly danced over the cracked, grimy sidewalks. She hardly paid attention to the trash in the gutters, the tattered curtains in rundown apartments, or the endless graffiti scarring every cement wall. Nothing could spoil the elation she felt—this first, tiny, fragile bud of . . . what? Love? Whatever it was, it felt warm and delicious, as bubbly as the fizz in her favorite carbonated drink. Lonnie Sandstrom was the most wonderful boy Maria had ever met—and he liked the way she sang! She would gladly sing for him forever—if only his smile could always be hers alone.

Maria refused to let thoughts of Lauren Pettegrew destroy this sudden, newfound joy. Lauren and Lonnie were merely friends, surely that was all. If they weren't just friends, why had he invited Maria to join them for lunch and praised her talent so openly? Lonnie had to be available, if for nothing more than to fill Maria's dreams.

Grandma Estrella commented on the light in Maria's eyes as soon as Maria entered the small, aroma-filled kitchen. "You look happy. You have good day at school?" the elderly woman said as she poured her special tomato sauce over a platter of chicken and rice.

Maria set her books on the counter. "Yes, it was a good day, and this is going to be the best school year ever!" Dreamily she removed two stoneware plates from the cupboard and carried them over to the table. "I like my classes, especially chorus. And I met some really neat people." Maria wanted to say more, but what she was feeling now couldn't be expressed easily in English or Spanish.

After dinner, as they lingered over their custard dessert, Maria urged, "Tell me about Grandpa Estrella, how you felt when you met him."

Her grandmother's face grew tender in a way Maria had never seen before. She looked past Maria as she breathed in Spanish, *"Ah, mi Miguel, mi esposo. Era todo un hombre. Tan alto y fuerte."*

"How did you meet Grandfather Estrella?"

"We meet in Mazatlan. At the festival. In springtime. Is celebration—like great carnival. We have rockets and masks and mariachis . . . and parades and grand balls and a bullfight. Your grandfather, such handsome man. He escort me everywhere. We dance and laugh . . . " As she remembered, the road map of lines on Grandmother Estrella's face softened; her pursed lips relaxed. A young girl's eyes gleamed from her wrinkled face. "I still have *cascarones* Miguel give me," she added, absently rubbing the slack, mottled skin on her left hand. "One *cascarone* have this ring inside."

"Your wedding ring?" cried Maria. She examined the worn silver ring on her grandmother's third finger. "How romantic!"

Grandma Estrella stood up with effort and limped over to the narrow buffet. She removed a faded box that filled the room with the musky fragrance of old perfume and handed it to Maria. "Remember?"

As Maria removed the lid her eyes settled on a nest of delicate dyed eggshells. "Yes! You showed me these when I was a little girl. They're filled with confetti from the festival. How I loved them!"

"They are the *cascarones* my Miguel give me long ago." She carefully removed a pale green egg. "This one hold my ring."

Maria felt her eyes brim with tears. "You loved Grandfather Estrella very much, didn't you?"

A quiet pause, then: "I love him still. He is my life."

Maria squeezed her grandmother's hand, aware of the crepe-papery frailness. "I love you, *Abuelita*." It was the first time since childhood Maria had used her special term of endearment, "Little Grandmother."

9

Maria started Tuesday morning in her favorite oversized shirt with patch pockets and a full circle skirt. But when she gazed in the mirror, she decided the outfit made her look like a bag lady. She quickly changed into her cowl-neck blouse with dolman sleeves and a pleated skirt. It still wasn't the look she wanted. Finally she settled on her beige georgette blouse and tattersall skirt. The outfit had cost her a month's allowance, but it was worth the price if Lonnie found her attractive.

Lonnie had been in Maria's thoughts from the moment she awoke. She could scarcely wait for fourth period chorus when she would see him again. Would he speak to her, walk her to lunch again . . . sit with her in the cafeteria?

Maria imagined the two of them lingering together in a cozy corner, talking raptly about music, sharing their secret hopes and dreams. With smug satisfaction she pictured Lauren Pettegrew slinking by, glaring jealously. Lonnie would be polite but firm: "I'm sorry, Lauren. I'm with Maria now."

But, to Maria's dismay, it wasn't like that at all. Lonnie was busy talking with other students before chorus class. Afterward, he left quickly, without a glance in her direction. She spotted him minutes later in the cafeteria. With Lauren. They were too engrossed in conversation to notice Maria passing by with her tray.

For the rest of the day Maria silently chided herself for being such a fool. Why had she assumed Lonnie liked her just because he was kind and friendly? *Maybe he didn't really think her voice was wonderful at all.* Maybe he had tossed her a few crumbs of praise because he pitied her! Maria felt too ashamed to face Lonnie again.

On Wednesday, when Lonnie grinned at her from across the room, Maria smiled back politely, then looked away. She wouldn't let herself be fooled again by Lonnie's friendly manner. And under no circumstances did she want him to guess how fond she was of him.

On Sunday morning, Maria went to church reluctantly. Once again she rode with Brett and Sarah and Sarah's twin brothers. The youngsters pretended they were alien creatures who spoke a strange, burpy language. When they had exhausted every variation of burp they could summon, they shouted in unison, "We are Teenage Mutant Ninja Turtles, and we've come to save the world!"

"Hey, you guys, save *us*," snapped Sarah, "by crawling back into your *shells*!"

Both boys also had colds which they shared generously with Maria. Maria mentally made a list of items to bring during future rides with Brett and Sarah—a raincoat to protect her clothes during Taco Bell lunches and a doctor's mask to ward off viruses spewed by elementary school space monsters.

As it turned out, Maria's discomfiting ride with the two contagious munchkins was well worth the trouble. Just before the pastor got up to speak, the choir director introduced Lonnie. He stood up with his shiny guitar and sang one of his own compositions—a bright, joyous song about giving one's heart to Jesus:

When you open your heart to Jesus
His Spirit steps right in.
He's your closest Friend forever,
Frees you from all guilt and sin.
He will never, ever leave you,
Never let you walk alone.
Christ will guide you through your heartaches
And see you safely home
To glory, glory, glory.

His glory will shine through you.
Glory, glory, glory.
Won't you give Him your love too?

Maria sat motionless, enthralled. She wasn't sure whether she had been mesmerized by Lonnie Sandstrom or by the Jesus of Lonnie's song. She knew only that she felt a response so deep, so painfully incisive, she couldn't ignore it. It erupted from some secret core of her own personhood. She had been born for this very moment, created to embrace the Someone Lonnie sang of. She couldn't sort out her barrage of feelings: She wanted Lonnie. She wanted Lonnie's joy. She wanted Lonnie's Jesus.

After the message, when the pastor gave a closing invitation to those desiring to accept Jesus into their lives, Maria was the first one up the aisle. A deacon in a brown tweed suit, with a shiny bald head and too-spicy after-shave, read to her from the Bible and prayed with her. Then she repeated a prayer after him, line by line, inviting Christ to be her personal Lord and Savior. Before she left, he wrote her name in a little book and handed it to her with a slow, paternal smile. She noticed perspiration winding down his jowls. The little room was stuffy. She was sweating too. She thanked the man politely and walked away with her little inscribed booklet, wishing it could have been Lonnie who prayed with her. Somehow, praying with a stocky, middle-aged stranger hadn't made her feel nearly as close to Jesus as Lonnie's song had.

As Maria rode home with Brett, Sarah, and Sarah's bickering brothers, she wondered if she really was a different person now. Had Jesus really come into her heart? Was she truly a new person . . . born again?

Sarah and Brett seemed to think so. They both chatted endlessly about how pleased they were with her decision. Sarah's brat-brothers didn't seem at all pleased. They were too busy trying to out-sneeze each other. Although she was ravenous, Maria swiftly declined Brett's offer of another Taco Bell lunch. "I'd better get home to my grandmother," she told him. "She'll have lunch waiting."

That wasn't exactly true. Maria had promised to fix Sunday dinner for Grandma Estrella later. Did her not-quite-accurate excuse constitute a lie? Or had she merely stretched the truth? Would God punish her for lying? He had just forgiven all her sins less than an hour ago. Would He start a new list now?

"Maria," said Sarah, "did you hear me? I asked if you want Brett and me to pick you up for the evening service." When Maria hesitated, Sarah glanced back knowingly at her brothers and added, "Don't worry. The two rabble-rousers will stay home tonight."

Maria grinned spontaneously. "In that case, I'd love a ride."

Lonnie led the singing as usual in the youth service that evening. Maria felt herself swept up in the rising tide of emotions that surged over the group. Even those with just-average voices sang with impressive energy. *They sing with such earnest joy because they're singing about Jesus,* Maria mused silently. She felt the same instinctive impulse within herself. Jesus seemed most real, most available, when she sang His praises.

After they finished singing an especially rousing chorus, Lonnie said with a sly buoyancy in his voice, "There's someone here I'd like you all to get to know. She has the voice of an angel. Maria, would you come up and sing a chorus with me?"

Maria looked around in sudden, heart-stopping horror. Did Lonnie really mean her? How could he do such a thing—put her on the spot like this, embarrass her in such a devastating way? She briskly shook her head and slunk down in her seat, praying for invisibility.

Sarah elbowed her and whispered loudly, "Go on up, Maria. We'd love to hear you sing."

With dazed, red-faced reluctance, Maria made her way to the front and stood trembling beside Lonnie. She felt warm, flushed. Her heart pounded loudly enough to provide drumbeat accompaniment to their duet. She wondered, would she swoon . . . faint dead away before everyone in the place? Would her voice break? Would any sound emerge, however weak and raspy?

Tentatively she joined Lonnie in his own beautifully penned song that he had sung that morning. The lyrics and tune were etched indelibly in Maria's mind. As the two of them completed the first stanza, Maria was struck by the rich, full sound of their perfectly blending voices. Lonnie heard it too. He flashed her his special smile as their voices rose as one, confident, in joyous harmony. When they finished the final phrase, everyone in the room broke into unrestrained applause.

Lonnie squeezed Maria's shoulder appreciatively. "We're going to have to sing together again real soon," he told her. "We sounded like dynamite."

Maria returned to her seat in a state of near euphoria. Her thoughts were short-circuited by heady sensations of awe and disbelief. She was only partly aware of Sarah patting her arm and congratulating her and Brett leaning over to compliment her. Suddenly, unexpectedly, Maria was just where she wanted to be—an accepted and admired member of the youth group. Surely she would have friends galore in the days ahead. And it seemed entirely possible that Lonnie Sandstrom would be counted among her closest companions!

10

At noon on Monday, as Maria pushed her tray through the cafeteria line, she heard a deep voice behind her ask, "Like some company?"

Her pulse quickened as she turned to look up at Lonnie. "Sure!"

"You know, Maria, since last night, I've been thinking a lot about you," he said as they found a table and set down their trays.

"Really? You have?" She noticed that he pulled back her chair and waited for her to sit down first. Hardly any guy did that anymore in these days of Women's Lib.

"I think we'd make a great team," Lonnie continued.

"You do?" she stammered. She felt a wonderful warmth spreading all the way to her toes.

"Yes. The way we sounded together last night, I'm sure we'd make a great singing team. Are you interested?"

The warmth faded. "Singing team? You mean, you want me to sing with you?"

"Right. We'd be terrific together."

"But, uh, sing where?"

"Oh, I'm booked almost every weekend at various churches in the area."

Maria shook her head. "I'm not ready to sing in public, Lonnie."

"Sure, you are. I'll help you."

"I'd be scared out of my wits."

"No, not once you get used to it. You're a natural, Maria." He bit into his sandwich and chewed thoughtfully. "Of course, we'd have to spend a lot of time together practicing. It might crimp your social life."

"My social life?" She muffled her laughter and resisted the urge to counter with, *What social life?* She thought about it for several moments. "Um, you say we'd have to spend a lot of time together? Like how much time?"

"Oh, a couple evenings a week, maybe, and an occasional Saturday or Sunday. I guess that's asking a lot, isn't it?"

"No," she said quickly. "It's not—it's—it's perfect. I'd love to sing with you, Lonnie."

"Great." He lifted his carton of milk to hers. "Let's drink a toast to the new singing sensation—Maria Estrella."

"And Lonnie Sandstrom," she added with a shy smile.

He grinned broadly. "Listen, Maria, we should celebrate."

"How?"

"There's a concert Friday night at the Performing Arts Center. The Pacific Symphony Orchestra is performing Mozart's *Requiem*."

"I—I'm not really familiar with classical music."

"That's OK. I know you'll like it. I just have a feeling about you, Maria."

She looked questioningly at him. "What feeling?"

"I mean, I don't know any other girl I'd feel comfortable asking to a concert like this. They'd want to hear Madonna or Janet Jackson or Milli Vanili. But you—you're different."

Maria felt that warm glow tingling under her skin again. "What time do you want me to be ready, Lonnie?"

"How about six? We'll have dinner first—my treat."

Friday evening was everything Maria hoped and dreamed it would be. Lonnie was stunningly handsome in his navy blue suit—a blond, blue-eyed Prince Charming who treated her like his princess. They had an early dinner at Reuben's Steakhouse, then headed for the concert. Afterward, they stopped at Big Boy's for strawberry pie.

"Strawberry pie is my absolute most favorite dessert," Maria confided as she speared a huge, juicy red berry crowned with swirls of whipped cream.

"Mine too," said Lonnie, "next to hot fudge sundaes."

Maria rolled her eyes longingly. "I forgot hot fudge sundaes."

"Next time," he promised. "So, tell me, how'd you like the concert?"

She smiled dreamily. "It was beautiful. I'll never forget tonight."

"The orchestra was in good form, don't you think? Of course, in the beginning, the cellos overwhelmed the woodwinds a bit, but all in all, they played with real sensitivity and excitement."

Maria gazed admiringly at Lonnie. "I wish I understood it all as well as you do. All I can say for certain is, I liked it."

"That's what counts." Lonnie poked absently at his pie crust. "Actually, I guess I was laying it on a little thick. If I talked music like this with anyone else, they'd think I was a dweeb or something."

"No, they wouldn't. They'd be impressed. How do you know it so well?"

He chuckled self-consciously. "My mom. She was one of these mothers who played classical music when she was pregnant so her baby would be born an accomplished musician."

Maria giggled. "Really? So instead of playing with blocks, you played 'Chopsticks'?"

"Something like that."

"I wish I could play the piano well," Maria said wistfully.

"Have you ever had lessons?"

"No. I play by ear, but I wish I could read the notes."

"Maybe someday you will. Maybe I can teach you when we practice our songs together."

"Would you? I can't wait."

"How about tomorrow afternoon at my house? I want to show you some sheet music and try some songs together."

Maria felt a tiny shiver travel down her spine. "How soon will we have to sing—in public?"

"A week from Sunday. We're scheduled for the First Christian Church over on Bellflower."

"That soon? You're a fast worker."

He smiled. "In some ways, I guess I am—when it counts."

"I honestly don't know if I'll be ready, Lonnie. I'd die if I embarrassed you."

He reached across the table and squeezed her hand. "You could never embarrass me, Maria. I know everybody will fall in love with your voice just as I have."

The warmth of Lonnie's hand sent tingles along Maria's wrist. Silently she yearned, *Oh, Lonnie, not just my voice. If only you could fall in love with ME!*

11

"Trick or treat!" Sarah Wilms stood in Maria's open doorway, wearing her plaid flannel shirt and jeans, a navy sweater tossed loosely around her shoulders. Behind her, two lumpy black globs stood in the shadows, each dragging a huge white pillowcase.

"What is this?" Maria laughed.

"I'm escorting my darling brothers around for Halloween. We've already covered my neighborhood, so we thought we'd try yours. These little bandits are out for all the loot they can get."

Maria leaned over and whispered, "What are they supposed to be?"

"Raisins."

"You're kidding!"

"No. Mom vetoed their first, second, and third choices, so they settled on raisins. Mom got the idea from the TV commercial. You know, the California raisins. She sewed a couple of black plastic trash sacks over black tights."

"Well, they certainly look . . . unique."

Sarah nodded. "So how about joining us in our moonlight trek?"

"Go trick or treating? I haven't done that since I was ten!"

"Not trick or treating. We'll just stand by the curb and watch while my brothers run up to each door. I know it sounds like a real pain, but my mom said I gotta stand patrol. Otherwise,

59

these two raisins would be out soaping windows or letting air out of tires.''

"Well, since it's for a good cause," said Maria. "Just let me grab a jacket and tell my grandmother.''

Maria found the chill October night invigorating. The air was fragrant with the nutty-toasty aroma of fires in chimneys being used for the first time in more than half a year. The usual drab neighborhood was suddenly inhabited by groups of colorful, prowling, pint-size creatures with goodie bags, escorted by harried, watchful parents.

As Willie and Wally lumbered up to each door in a raisin-like, roly-poly galumph, Maria and Sarah followed at a leisurely pace. They chatted about the latest school and church activities, about friends, would-be friends, and those who would be more than friends—if Sarah and Maria had their way.

"How's Lonnie?" Sarah ventured as the twins raced each other to a corner house.

Maria looked quickly at her friend. "Lonnie's fine, I guess. Why do you ask?''

"I heard you two have been singing together at churches in the area.''

"A few.''

"That's great. I loved the song you and Lonnie sang in church the night you were baptized and joined the church. I had a feeling Lonnie wrote the song just for you.''

Maria smiled. "He did. It was about a singer finally having a reason to sing . . . because of Jesus.''

"It was beautiful, Maria." Sarah pulled her sweater closer around her shoulders. "I guess you like singing with Lonnie.''

"I love it," said Maria. "It's opened a whole new world to me." She paused, reflecting. "At first I was scared to death to sing in front of people. But Lonnie has been so patient and encouraging. The last time we sang I hardly got stage fright at all.''

"You like him a lot, don't you?''

"Lonnie? Of course. We're good friends.''

"I mean more than that," said Sarah slyly.

Maria forced back a nervous laugh. "What are you talking about?''

"You can level with me. Your face beams when you're with him."

"It shows that much?"

"Sure does. I'm good at reading people. But I'm not the only one who's noticed."

"What do you mean? Has someone said something?"

"You might say the church grapevine has been working overtime lately, Maria. Come on, don't you know what I'm talking about? Lauren and Company—the powers that be at Community Bible."

"Sarah, that's a weird thing to say," protested Maria.

Before Sarah could respond, the twins scrambled up to them, panting with glee. "The corner house just gave us popcorn balls and big Baby Ruths," exclaimed Wally, his plastic costume rippling as he waved excitedly.

"Will you go up and get us doubles?" begged Willie, bouncing up and down on his knobby legs.

"I will not," Sarah said testily. "I don't even have a costume."

"Just make a face," said Wally, "and they'll never know the difference."

"Get out of here, you two, before I bake you in a raisin cookie!"

The twins bounded away in their lumpish, bobbing bags. Maria and Sarah sauntered on, keeping a respectable distance between themselves and the frisky Super Raisins.

"I was about to say something before we were so rudely interrupted," Sarah said, her voice lacking its usual easygoing tone.

"Is something wrong?" Maria asked.

"Not exactly. I just feel I should . . . warn you."

"Warn me? About what?"

"Not what. *Whom.* Lauren, Denise, and some of the other girls aren't happy about the attention Lonnie is giving you."

"They told you that?"

"Of course not. I'm not in their league—their little clique. But I've heard things. They intend to get even with you, Maria."

"But I haven't done anything!"

"Don't be so dense, Maria. Lonnie is the most popular and eligible guy in our church. Any gal would give her Cover Girl complexion to be Lonnie's lady."

"But Lonnie doesn't have a special girl," argued Maria. "Sure, he goes around with Lauren, but he pays attention to all the girls."

"That's the beauty of it. Every girl thinks she has a chance with Lonnie. Of course, classy, charming Lauren merely waves a painted fingernail and everyone bows at her feet, so she gets first dibs on Lonnie. The other girls respect her claim, so there's no problem. At least, there wasn't until you came along."

"Does Lonnie know about this—this game plan of Lauren's?"

Sarah's mouth dropped in amazement. "Are you kidding, Maria? He wouldn't believe it if you told him. He's a very upfront, friendly guy. He doesn't question people's motives or analyze their intentions. He thrives on being liked by everyone."

"Well, Lonnie and I are just friends. Lauren must know that."

"She's keeping her claws in so far, but she's watching you like a cat. One wrong move and—"

"Oh, Sarah, really! I'm no threat to Lauren. The only reason I'm accepted by Lonnie or the rest of the group is because I can sing. Otherwise, I'd still be an outsider."

Sarah was silent. Maria wished Sarah would argue the point and reassure her she was liked simply for herself. Until now, Maria hadn't consciously admitted that her voice had earned her her coveted position in the in-crowd at church. "Are you sure your suspicions aren't just sour grapes?" challenged Maria.

Sarah looked around in mock bafflement. "Sour grapes? What are we talking about—my brothers, the raisins?"

"Of course not. I just think you're exaggerating things . . . seeing problems where there aren't any."

Sarah shrugged her broad, bony shoulders. "OK, Maria. Just wait and see what happens if Lonnie ever takes more than a brotherly interest in you!"

Sarah's gloomy warning produced just the opposite result. Maria felt a tickle rise from her stomach to her throat. She began to laugh deliriously. "Oh, Sarah, if only Lonnie would like me that way!"

Sarah clasped Maria's arm urgently. "I knew it! You're in love with him, aren't you, Maria?"

"Hopelessly," Maria confessed between fits of giggles.

Sarah began to laugh, too. They held on to each other, their frames shaking with great gales of laughter. "I'm the only one who's not madly in love with Lonnie Sandstrom," Sarah gasped.

"I know," cried Maria, wiping the silly tears from her eyes. "Because you're crazy in love with Brett Burkhard."

Sarah swallowed her laughter in one startled gulp. "I am?"

"Of course," Maria panted. "I see it from the back seat every time I ride with you two—even with your goofy brothers playing alien invaders across me."

"That's ridiculous, Maria. Brett is homely and insufferably intellectual and he avoids girls like the plague."

"Not you. He likes you, Sarah. He just doesn't know it yet."

Sarah brightened. "Maybe you're right, Maria. I guess I *am* crazy about him. But I never thought about the two of us being anything but friends."

"I guess this has been an enlightening evening for both of us," said Maria, raising her chin haughtily as she mimicked Lauren's lofty tone.

Sarah chuckled. "A perfect imitation." She paused and looked around in sudden panic. "Where are the twins?"

"They were just at that house on the left," Maria said, pointing. "They couldn't have gotten far."

"You don't know Willie and Wally," Sarah called back as she darted into the street. "I don't see them anywhere, Maria!"

Maria caught up with her friend and placed a soothing arm around her shoulder. "Don't worry, Sarah. We'll find them. They're probably just playing a little Halloween prank on us."

"That's what I'm afraid of," moaned Sarah. They walked up one block, then another, calling the twins by name. There was no response. They stopped a myriad motley little creatures of the night who shoved and squealed, "Trick or treat," in decibels geared to shatter eardrums.

"Have you seen two rather large, plump raisins?" they asked at a multitude of doors. "Well, not large really," they explained lamely. "Large for raisins, but short for human beings." No matter how they inquired, they were met by cold stares and what-are-you-pulling expressions. One puffy-faced lady stuck caramel apples in their hands and slammed the door, mumbling something about how old trick-or-treaters were getting these days. Several people rattled off greetings in Spanish and insisted the girls help themselves to bowls of Tootsie Rolls and candy corn.

After nearly a half hour of futile searching, Sarah shook her head in despair. "Oh, Maria, my mom will kill me for losing the twins. She's always saying she's going to take them out and lose them, but now I've actually done it!"

"They'll be all right. They're just having a little harmless fun—"

"Nothing is harmless about the twins. They're in trouble, I know it. I never should have let Brett drop us off in this neighborhood!"

Maria felt a sudden coolness wash over her. "What do you mean . . . *this* neighborhood?"

Sarah stopped and looked blankly at her. "Well, you must know. It's dangerous around here. It's full of dopers and gangs and—"

"And poor Latinos like my grandmother and me?"

The two girls stared at each other in stark, numb silence. Within moments their stony expressions crumbled. They clasped each other brokenly. "I'm sorry, Maria. I didn't mean it that way. You're my best friend!"

"I didn't mean it either. I was just being defensive."

They walked back to Maria's house. "I'll have to call my mother," lamented Sarah. "She'll call the police. They'll put out a dragnet. It'll be in the papers and on TV." She sighed melodramatically. "The FBI will set up a stakeout and interrogate everyone we've ever known. Our lives will be disrupted for months; maybe we'll even appear on 'Unsolved Mysteries,' but it'll be worth it if only we find my poor little brothers—"

"Sarah! Sa-RAH!" It was the familiar, high-pitched scream of the twins. They were sitting on Maria's porch, one on each side of a shadowed, muscular young man.

Maria approached cautiously, peering through the darkness at the stranger. "Enrique Fernandez!" she exclaimed in relief.

He stood up, jerking the boys upright by the napes of their wrinkled necks. "Do these two fruitcakes belong to you?"

Maria gestured awkwardly toward Sarah. "They're hers."

"My brothers," she said quickly. "Are they hurt?"

"Not yet," Enrique said, his accented voice clipped. He removed a cigarette from his lips and exhaled slowly. "But they came near to getting leveled."

"You mean they almost got hit by a car?" cried Sarah, pulling the cherub-faced youngsters into her arms.

"Not exactly," growled Enrique. "I caught them letting the air out of a tire a few blocks from here." He looked meaningfully at Maria. "It's a Chevy. It belongs to Raul Naranjo."

She covered her mouth with her hands. "Oh, no! Does Raul know?"

"Who's Raul Naranjo?" asked Sarah.

"You don't want to know him," Maria whispered. She turned back to Enrique and asked urgently, "Is Raul looking for the boys?"

"Nah. He doesn't know. I got the kids out of there fast. He'll figure it was a rival gang. It'll mean trouble for someone."

Maria looked at Enrique in amazement. "Why did you rescue the boys?"

He shrugged. "They said they knew you. Said you were their favorite person."

Maria choked involuntarily. Beatific smiles beamed from the twins' pudgy faces as they folded their hands innocently over their shiny raisin-bellies.

The facts of the situation were just beginning to dawn on Sarah. "You mean, while we were out searching for you two boys—worried sick, terrified that you might be kidnapped or dead—you two loonies were running around playing pranks? Why, if I were your mother, I'd blister you both!" She shook the youngsters until they bounced on their round, padded bottoms. "I'm going to go call Brett. You boys are going home this instant!" she declared, pushing them toward Maria's front door.

Enrique turned to Maria and took her hand. "I'm still waiting, pretty lady, for our night out for pizza. Don't you forget me."

Maria pulled her hand away, flustered. She caught a glimpse of the horrified expression on Sarah's face. "I—I really didn't promise anything, Enrique," she stammered. "I'm very busy these days."

Enrique drew in on his cigarette, then ambled toward the street in a deliberate swagger. *"Adios, bonita,"* he said in a slow, Spanish drawl. "If you need me, I'm easy to find."

When he had gone, Sarah drew Maria away from the twins and whispered confidentially, "I don't know who that man is, Maria, but you'd better stay away from him. He looks like a gangster. And did you notice the strange smell of his cigarette? I'm sure it was marijuana. He may be dangerous, Maria."

Maria shrugged. "He's just a neighbor, Sarah. He works for my grandmother sometimes. I certainly don't plan to date him."

Even as she spoke, Maria felt vaguely guilty for not defending Enrique. In fact, she hadn't dared admit it to herself until now, but she rather liked Enrique Fernandez in a puzzling way. This wasn't the first time he had come to her rescue in unexpected circumstances. And no matter how Maria resisted the idea, Enrique was a Latino like herself. She was just beginning to be aware of the unspoken bond between them that even her friend Sarah, an Anglo, would never quite understand.

12

Maria stood in Alvarez's Christmas tree lot, sizing up a stubby blue spruce. The tree was small but nicely shaped, with lots of lush, green branches. It would fit perfectly in Grandma Estrella's little living room. Best of all, it was only eight dollars.

"Now if I can just figure out how to get it home," she mused aloud.

"We don't deliver," snapped a wizened little Cuban whose brown whiskered chin resembled the spiky texture of a coconut.

"I'll take it anyway," Maria announced, "and drag it home myself."

But a half hour later, Maria questioned her foolhardy decision as she sank against a cinder block wall with her recalcitrant tree. She still had four blocks to go to reach home. She could leave the tree and go for help. But then she noticed a handful of little berry-faced boys with wide, olive-black eyes watching from behind a weathered fence. They were waiting for her to grow tired and forsake her cumbersome prize. Perhaps stealing was the only way they would have a tree for Christmas. But Maria wasn't about to forfeit hers, not after doling out eight dollars! She would stay with her tree even if it meant camping on this corner all night.

Already the slanting rays of the sun were growing evening-cool. Maria shivered involuntarily. "Oh, what am I going to do now?" she said aloud.

"Hey, pretty lady, you talking to a tree?"

Maria whirled around and looked sheepishly into the face of Enrique Fernandez. He smiled down with his usual penetrating gaze. His thick black hair curled over his forehead and trailed down his neck. "You scared me," she gasped.

"You scared *me*. I figured you had turned loco, having a little chat with that tree."

Maria brushed off her jeans. "I can't get it home. It's too heavy."

Enrique grinned. "That's no problem. You carry my package and I'll carry yours." He handed Maria a Penney's sack and the brown cigarette he had been smoking. "Help yourself, babe. It's good stuff."

"I don't smoke," Maria said curtly. She held the cigarette gingerly, as if it might suddenly rear up and devour her hand. "It's not a regular one, is it?"

"It's better, foxy lady," said Enrique, hoisting Maria's tree onto his shoulder. "But don't worry. It's no crack . . . no PCP. It's just Mary Jane."

"I don't do drugs," said Maria.

"Hey, take just one drag. Grass mellows you out, makes you feel real good."

Maria handed the reefer back to him. "I don't need it," she said firmly.

"Well, when you do need a joint, you come to Enrique. I'll see that you get the pure stuff, none of that junk mixed in."

Maria glanced around uneasily. What if a squad of policemen converged on them now? Would they arrest Maria for associating with a doper? The darkening street was empty. No one in sight. Maria sighed with relief. She held up Enrique's sack she was carrying. "What's this—a Christmas present?"

He nodded. "It's a lamb. Feel it. It's all white and soft like a baby. I got it for my sister Rita."

"Your little sister?"

"No, she's my big sis. She's pregnant. And is she *ever* big!" he laughed. "The baby's not due till April, but she already looks like a house. I kid her. I say, 'You're gonna outdo Mama.' None of this one baby at a time bit; she's gonna have all six at once!"

"Is she really having more than one baby?"

Enrique shifted the tree to his other shoulder. "I don't know. She won't go to a doctor. I guess she feels funny—you know, not being married. I woulda broke the guy's arm to get him to the altar, but he took off. A real scum."

"It must be awfully hard for your sister."

Enrique shrugged. He was walking with a slight stoop now under the weight of the tree. "She cries a lot," he said. "That's why I got her the present, so she'll know she won't be sad and lonely forever. Soon she'll have her own little baby to love her." His voice took on a guarded pride. "It'll be Mama's first grandchild."

"I'd like to see the baby when it comes," said Maria.

"Sure. Rita would like that. I told her about you. I think you would like each other."

"She's older, isn't she?"

"Nineteen, but she looks younger. You come visit her, Maria. She's usually stuck at home with our little brothers. She gets real down sometimes."

They reached Grandma Estrella's house shortly after dusk. Enrique carried the tree inside and set it in the corner near the piano, as Maria directed.

"Ah, *chicos,* is beautiful!" her grandmother exclaimed, dabbing her eyes with her handkerchief.

Maria turned privately to Enrique. "My grandmother hasn't had a real Christmas tree since my grandfather died."

"What good is tree when I am only one here?"

Maria slipped her arm around the frail woman. *"Abuelita,* this Christmas is going to be special." She looked over at Enrique. "My dad is coming. The three of us will be together again."

"Your old man's coming for Christmas?" echoed Enrique. "That's great." His voice took on a hint of pessimism as he added, "Just don't expect too much from him, Maria."

She gave him a peevish glance. Who was he to dampen her spirits just when things were going well? Before she could offer a retort, Grandma Estrella said, *"Por favor,* you stay for dinner, Enrique. We have plenty tamales and rice. Tell him to stay, Maria."

Maria nodded half-heartedly. Lonnie was picking her up later for Madrigal Singers practice. It would never do for him to find her in the company of Enrique Fernandez! Maria squared her shoulders and nodded toward the kitchen. "Come on, Enrique. Let's eat right away. I'm starved!"

Maria managed to say a tense, hurried good-bye to Enrique just minutes before Lonnie arrived. Lonnie, with his wholesome, blond good looks, quiet manner, and even temper, was a striking contrast to the dark, volatile Enrique. Lonnie greeted Grandma Estrella warmly, inquired about her health, admired the Christmas tree, and complimented Maria on her new winter jacket.

In the car, all the way to the civic auditorium, Lonnie and Maria kept up an animated conversation about music, chorus class, and Madrigal Singers. They would be rehearsing with groups from a dozen other high schools for a city-wide concert on Christmas Eve. At ten, after the rehearsal, they stopped by a Marie Callender's restaurant for homemade potato cheese soup and boysenberry pie.

"So what are you doing for Christmas?" Lonnie asked as Maria savored a mouthful of pie.

"Nothing special," she replied between bites. She thought about her father arriving from Colorado on Christmas Eve, but she couldn't share that good news with Lonnie. Not after she had unthinkingly led him to believe her father was dead.

"We're having scads of relatives over for the holidays," said Lonnie, "but maybe I can get by to see you for a few minutes on Christmas day."

"Oh, that isn't necessary," Maria said quickly. "Grandmother and I may be attending a party at the senior citizens' recreation center." How easily a lie rolled from her lips!

"That doesn't sound like much fun."

"Oh, I don't mind. The people are . . . interesting."

"Well, when do you plan to decorate your tree?"

"I don't know. I'm not even sure Grandmother has lights and decorations."

"We have extras at my house. I'll bring them over. Is tomorrow evening OK?"

Maria nodded. "It'll give us one more chance to practice our duet for Sunday morning. I may even bake some Christmas cookies."

"Way to go! We could even decorate cookies to hang on the tree. My mom does that every year."

"And I could make popcorn to string," suggested Maria.

Lonnie grinned. "I've never strung popcorn, but I'm willing to try."

"We'll make Grandmother's house look like an old-fashioned Christmas," she enthused.

By the time Lonnie walked Maria to her door, the December night crackled with a biting chill. Lonnie lifted his overcoat collar and clasped Maria's cold fingers. Before she slipped inside the silent house, Lonnie leaned over casually and brushed her lips with a kiss.

Maria would forever remember the warmth and lightness of that kiss, the scent of Lonnie's after-shave, the Dentyne sweetness of his breath. But the moment was quickly marred. As Lonnie strolled back to his car, a battered, rust-encrusted VW roared up the street, its radio blaring acid rock, and screeched to a stop beside Lonnie's vehicle. A young, leather-jacketed Latino leaned out of the window and called, "Hey, gringo, you want some crack? Only thirty dollars!"

Lonnie glared at the stranger. "No way, man."

The automobile lurched forward while its occupants spewed profanity. Then it sped away with a searing, metallic roar.

Lonnie turned around and gazed in dismay at Maria. "You and your grandmother should move away from here," he warned, a tremor in his voice. "It's too dangerous for decent people. Those gangs come straight from the devil!"

Maria winced, wondering what Lonnie would say if he knew she counted similar barrio "devils" among her personal friends?

13

On Christmas Eve morning, Maria walked to Enrique's house with a gift from Grandma Estrella for Rita's unborn baby. Maria had been reluctant to deliver the present, today of all days. She didn't even know Rita Fernandez, and there was still so much work to do at home. But how could she refuse her dear *Abuelita*'s request?

Rita herself opened the door to Maria. She was a short, pretty brunette with large, sable, doe-sad eyes and a mass of charcoal hair cascading over her shoulders. She wore a faded housedress that swelled noticeably at her middle. She stared blankly at Maria, then broke into a spontaneous smile when Maria introduced herself.

"I guess I should have come by sooner," said Maria politely. "We live so close and haven't even gotten acquainted."

"I don't get out much lately," said Rita, leading Maria inside. "I take care of the younger boys while Mama works."

"That doesn't sound like much fun," noted Maria.

Rita grimaced. "It beats Mama's job. She cleans toilets in a fleabag hotel."

Maria glanced around at the cramped, untidy rooms and wondered how so many people managed to live here together. The air had a pungent odor—the combined smells of chili peppers, onions, mildew—and marijuana?

In one corner, two small, pajama-clad boys sat watching a flickering, black and white TV. Rita turned down the sound, ignoring the boys' loud protests, and removed several shirts and magazines from the worn sofa. "Sit down, Maria. Want a Coke or something?"

"No, thanks. I can't stay long. My grandmother wanted me to bring this over to you." She handed Rita the tissue-wrapped package. "It's for the baby."

"Oh, Maria, this is my baby's first present!" Rita caught herself and laughed. "No, it's the second. Enrique bought a little lamb."

"I know. I saw it. It's darling."

"Oh, and so is this!" exclaimed Rita, holding up a downy, pastel quilt.

"Grandmother made it."

"My baby will love it! Rita gave Maria a spontaneous hug. "Please, I have sweet tamales with raisins and cinnamon. We must celebrate!"

"No, really, I can't," said Maria, going to the door. "My father is arriving this afternoon, and I'm singing in a concert tonight. I can't believe it's already Christmas Eve. I still have presents to wrap."

In the doorway Rita clasped Maria's hand warmly. "Merry Christmas, Maria. You come back again soon. I want us to be friends."

"I'd like that too, Rita," Maria replied as she started down the narrow steps. Surprisingly, Maria meant it. She genuinely liked Rita Fernandez.

Maria nearly ran the two blocks home. What if her father had arrived early? There were still sheets to change, sinks to scrub, and chickens to bake. Maria had given Grandma Estrella strict orders to leave the hard tasks for her, but Maria still had to shower and press her dress for the concert at seven.

The thought of her father seeing her on stage tonight sent a fresh thrill of anticipation along Maria's spine. How she wanted him to be proud of her! Everything had to be perfect for her father who was finally coming home!

Maria practiced her solo parts for the Christmas cantata while she showered. Then, as she shampooed her hair, she said aloud, "Thank You, Jesus, for Christmas. Thank You for letting Lonnie like me. Thank You for bringing my dad home to us."

José Estrella arrived just as Maria finished swirling mascara on her lashes. She hurriedly put away her makeup and curling iron, took one last glance in the mirror, then ran to the door to greet him. He looked impressive in his blue suit—a big-boned, barrel-chested man. His soot-black hair was trimmed neatly around his ears; his grin was as wide as ever. He swept Maria up in his arms and swung her around. "Hey, my little girl's all grown up!" he boomed.

"She is very good girl," Grandma Estrella praised.

José embraced them both at once and walked them over to the couch. "Before I unpack a thing or help myself to some coffee, I just want to collapse in a chair." After they had chatted for several minutes, Maria could contain her excitement no longer.

"Papa, I'm singing tonight in the city-wide Christmas concert. I have two solo parts!"

"That's wonderful, sweetheart. I always did say you had a voice like an angel. I remember how you used to sing for your mama . . . " His voice trailed off; the gleam in his eyes faded.

"I want you to come, Papa. You and Grandmother."

Her father rubbed his large hand over his face, massaging his temples in a gesture of weariness. "I don't know, Maria. I've driven all day. I'm dead tired."

"Oh, please, Papa!"

"I'm not sure your grandmother could sit that long with her arthritis."

"My arthritis hurt always," said Grandma Estrella. "No matter if I sit here or other place."

José stood up and walked across the room to the window. "Say, Maria, did you see my new car? A spanking new Buick. Got it just last month."

Maria followed his gaze out the window. The car was nice, but it didn't interest her now. "What about the concert, Papa?"

"I told you, I'm beat, and it's too hard for your grandmother to go out. You'll be singing again, won't you? You wrote about all the duets you're doing with that fellow—"

"Lonnie Sandstrom."

"OK, so I'll catch the two of you some other time while I'm here."

Maria's shoulders sank dejectedly. How could she tell her father that she didn't dare introduce him to Lonnie, that Lonnie believed her father was dead? She couldn't even allow the two of them to meet tonight when Lonnie picked her up for the concert.

Lonnie and his parents arrived early. Maria rushed outside and climbed into the car before Lonnie could turn off the engine. "That's what I call prompt," he teased. "But shouldn't I run in and say hello to your grandmother? It's Christmas Eve."

"She's not feeling well," Maria lied.

"I'm sorry. Maybe you shouldn't leave her alone."

"Oh, no, she'll be fine. It's nothing serious." Guilt feelings surged over Maria, but she pushed them away, concentrating instead on the evening to come. She would sing her very best ever!

After the concert, amid a standing ovation and swarms of happy-weepy choristers, Lonnie and Maria found each other and embraced in joyous relief. "You were sensational," he told her.

"So were you," she cried.

"Let's celebrate at my house," he suggested. "Maybe fix popcorn and hot chocolate."

"Sounds perfect," said Maria.

"We won't stay long," he assured her. "I know you don't like leaving your grandmother alone and ill on Christmas Eve."

Maria was about to say, "It's OK, my dad's there," but she caught herself and said instead, "Grandma probably went to bed early."

Lonnie slipped his arm around her as they walked to the car. "I'm glad there's no hurry to get you home," he whispered.

At the car, Mr. and Mrs. Sandstrom greeted Maria warmly. Lonnie helped her into the front seat, taking care not to crush her delicate pastel evening dress. "You sang beautifully, Maria," said Mrs. Sandstrom. "You really should consider a professional career in music."

Maria smiled shyly. "I'd like to . . . if I can afford to go to college someday."

"There are scholarships, you know," suggested Mr. Sandstrom, "especially for someone as talented as you."

Lonnie reached over and squeezed her hand. "See? My folks are in your corner all the way."

The Sandstrom home was a well-kept two-story house in an older residential section of Downey. Maria adored the homey but elegant New England furnishings—a lullaby-blue carpet, plush armchairs and loveseat, and a quaint birch droplid desk. While Mr. Sandstrom put a log in the fireplace, Mrs. Sandstrom served fruitcake and hot cider. With a twinkle in his eyes, Lonnie removed a package from under the flocked fir tree and handed it to Maria. "Merry Christmas," he said, kissing her cheek.

Maria carefully opened the gold foil-wrapped gift and held up a strand of gleaming white pearls. "Oh, Lonnie, they're beautiful!"

"They're cultured pearls," said Lonnie. With a hint of merriment he added, "I guess that means they've got real *class*."

Maria laughed easily, then waited while Lonnie fastened the necklace around her neck. "You shouldn't have spent so much, Lonnie."

He sat beside her on the velvet loveseat. "I wanted you to know you're special to me, Maria." He glanced around. They were alone for the moment. In a soft, earnest voice, he said, "I want you to be my girl, Maria."

Her heart pounded maddeningly. "But—what about Lauren?"

He looked puzzled. "Lauren? Why would you ask about her?"

"You two were always together. I thought . . ."

"Lauren has never been anything more than a friend, Maria. She knows that."

"I—I figured you two were in love—"

"Lauren and I? Oh, Maria, Lauren is bright and brassy and fun to be with, but she's not someone to take seriously." When Maria looked doubtful, Lonnie persisted, "Life is one big carnival for Lauren, a constant party. I could never live that way. I wouldn't want to. I want a girl who's sincere, who's open and honest with me, not always flirty and playing games."

He tipped Maria's chin toward him. "I want a girl like you, Maria." He lowered his head to hers and kissed her with exquisite tenderness. Maria responded, instinctively returning the kiss. Christmas Eve had become a night of blissful enchantment.

Becoming Lonnie's girl softened Maria's pain at facing her first Christmas without her mother. Secretly, she had dreaded the day, tried to put it out of her mind, concentrating instead on the Christmas Eve concert and her father's visit.

When Maria awoke on Christmas morning, memories of Christmases past assailed her with unexpected force—recollections of Maria and her mother wrapping gifts, decorating the tree, baking Christmas cookies. She almost heard her mother's laughter, her sweet soprano voice singing "Silent Night." The sounds and images remained vivid in Maria's mind as she passed the bittersweet hours of Christmas with her father and grandmother.

In the lull following Christmas dinner, Maria stole to her room and sat on her bed studying her mother's picture. She clasped the photograph against her chest and wept soundlessly until her tears were spent. Then she dried her eyes and whispered a prayer, thankful for the one steady gleam of light in her heart— the Lord Jesus. This year He was more to her than just a baby in a manger. He was her Savior, and every day He was becoming more her friend.

As the final hours of Christmas day faded, Maria resolved anew to put the past behind her, to think only of the future and the life she and her father could build together. Hadn't Papa hinted shortly after his arrival that he had special plans to discuss with her? Maybe this time he had come to California to stay.

It wasn't until two days after Christmas that her father mentioned again his mysterious plans. "We have some important things to talk over, Maria," he told her after breakfast. "I've got some news for you."

"Good news?" she ventured.

He flashed an inscrutable grin. "I think so."

"Well, tell me!"

"How about if I take my best girl out to a fancy restaurant for dinner? We can chat all we like, nice and private, just the two of us."

"What about Grandma Estrella?"

"She won't mind. She and I talked the other night while you were at the concert. She's the one who suggested we spend some time together."

77

Maria nodded, pleased. "Grandmother would think of that."

"All right, it's settled. Dinner at seven. I'll dust off my best duds and you trot out your fanciest dress."

Maria's excitement bubbled like spring water. "Where are we going?"

"To a dandy little place with the best Mexican food you ever tasted. Your mama and I used to go there in our courting days."

That evening, as Maria and her father entered the quaint, white stucco restaurant with its colorful pottery and hand-woven tapestries, she already knew she adored La Casita—if for no other reason than because it was here her father had romanced her mother. Perhaps years ago they had sat at this very carved oak table and watched the vibrant, fast-stepping folkloric dancers or listened raptly to the handsome, strolling mariachis. Maria tried to imagine what her parents looked like then, how they felt, and what they talked about. How happy they must have been!

"Well, Maria, my little dreamer," said Jose. "You are so far away."

She laughed lightly, embarrassed. "I was thinking about you and Mama. She must have loved coming here, being with you."

"Yes, she did," Jose mused, his eyes bright with memories. His expression tightened as he added, "But those days are gone, Maria."

She looked away, swallowing a lump in her throat. "Do you go to the cemetery often, Papa?"

Her father hesitated. A nerve in his cheek twitched slightly. "No, Maria. I—I haven't been since the funeral."

She stared at him in disbelief. "Not since the funeral? How could you not go?"

Jose cracked his knuckles. Tiny beads of perspiration dotted his upper lip. "It hurts, Maria. You should understand that."

"If I were home, I would go to the cemetery every day. I would bring Mama flowers and make sure the grass wasn't growing too tall."

"It wouldn't bring Mama back, Maria. We have to go on without her, both of us."

Maria nodded. "Is that what you want to talk about? Are you moving to California to be with Grandmother and me?"

Jose's eyes registered surprise. "Why would you think that?"

"You said you had plans to discuss with me."

Jose dipped a tortilla chip into the hot sauce. "I have made some plans, Maria. I hope you'll be happy about them."

She shrugged, puzzled. "Why wouldn't I be?"

A red-jacketed waiter brought the *carne asada* Jose had ordered. He served it with a flourish, then handed Maria her taco salad. "More avocado or sour cream, *señorita?*"

"No, everything's fine, thank you." She turned back to her father with a growing sense of urgency. "What *are* your plans, Papa?"

He seemed engrossed in cutting his steak. Finally he said, almost under his breath, "I've met someone, Maria."

She looked blankly at him. "Met someone?"

"A very nice lady. Her name is Angela. She's Italian, about twenty-eight. Very pretty. A widow with two small children."

"So?"

The tendons in Jose's neck tightened. He took out his handkerchief and wiped his upper lip. "We're seeing each other, Maria." He reached across the table for her hand. "You would like her . . ."

Maria withdrew her hand. "How could you see someone so soon after Mama?"

"It's been almost a year, Maria."

"No one could ever take Mama's place!"

Jose sat forward intently. "Angela and I are getting married."

"No! No, no, no!" Maria pushed back her chair and stood up.

"Wait, Maria," said Jose. "You haven't finished your dinner."

She stumbled two tables away, her vision blurred by tears. Her father followed and caught her in his arms. "It'll work out, Maria. Please believe me!"

"I—I suppose you expect me to step right into your ready-made family as if Mama never even existed!" she cried.

"We haven't even set a date yet, Maria," said Jose. He hesitated. "But I think it would be best for Angela and me to be on our own for a while until we get used to being a family. It won't be easy with two little children in the house."

Maria felt herself crumbling inside. "You mean—you don't want me at all?"

"Just for a while, Maria. We'll need time to adjust. But you can come visit us this summer, maybe even help Angela plan the wedding."

"I thought the two of us were going to be a family," sobbed Maria.

Wordlessly, Jose led her back to their table. She sat down, wiping her eyes, feeling suddenly self-conscious. People were staring. She glanced around and caught her breath in dismay as she recognized a familiar face. Lauren Pettegrew with her parents at a corner table. Had she spotted Maria? Maria slunk down in her chair and covered her face with her hand. She couldn't possibly introduce Lauren to her father. He was supposed to be dead!

14

The last few days of December were bleak for Maria. Her father returned to Colorado with the breach between them unresolved. Just when Maria needed consolation, the telephone remained silent. Lonnie didn't call until New Year's Eve. Even then, he was strangely short on sympathy. He told her curtly he would pick her up as planned for the church watch-night service, but Maria sensed there was more he wanted to say. He sounded almost angry with her. Why? What had she done?

Or was it merely her imagination? No. Lonnie was unmistakably sullen during their drive to church. His words were clipped, edged with antagonism. Maria felt baffled, dismayed. Had Lonnie stopped caring for her? Was he trying to tell her their relationship was over?

Maria's despair grew as the evening progressed. Lonnie ignored her completely. During refreshments, he took punch and cookies over to Lauren and sat with her and Denise. When he finally returned to Maria, she forced back her tears and said, "Please take me home, Lonnie."

"Now? The candlelight service is about to begin."

"If you don't take me, I'll catch the bus . . . or walk."

"Wait. I'll take you. I'll get our coats."

The drive home was as painfully silent as the drive to church had been. Maria was bursting with questions but too proud to voice her frustration. But as Lonnie approached her neighborhood, her pride dissolved. "What happened, Lonnie?" she asked plaintively. "What did I do wrong?"

Lonnie sat with his back rigid, his face like stone, his gaze focused on the road ahead. "You know what you did," he said sharply.

"I do not," she retorted. "I've never done anything to hurt you like you're hurting me now!"

"Oh, no? How about your romantic little dinner at La Casita a few nights ago?"

"La Casita? How did you know about that?" Even as she asked, Maria knew the answer. "Lauren! She told you she saw me there."

"You and your new boyfriend," Lonnie said thickly. "At first I figured Lauren was inventing stories out of spite or jealousy. But her parents saw you too. I hear you and this guy had quite a lovers' quarrel."

"It wasn't like that at all."

"Wasn't it? Since when did you start going around with older men?"

Angry tears coursed down Maria's cheeks. "How could you believe such a thing? How could you think I'd cheat on you?"

Lonnie gave her a desolate glance. "I thought you were different, Maria. I thought I could count on you."

She reached for the door handle. "Stop the car, Lonnie. I'll walk home from here."

"Don't be a fool. It's dangerous. Every creep in the county will be out on New Year's Eve."

"Anything's better than listening to your accusations," she cried, swinging open the door.

Lonnie slowed the automobile to a crawl. "Just tell me who you were out with, Maria."

Her throat constricted as she blurted, "I was with my father!" In one swift leap she sprang from the moving car. Her feet struck the pavement with jarring force. She nearly fell, then caught herself and regained her balance.

Lonnie swerved to the curb, braked, and jumped out. "Maria, come back!"

She couldn't face Lonnie now. She ran down the street toward the cheerless barrio dwellings. A few houses were still strung with Christmas lights—tiny beacons of color in a wash of somber blacks and grays. Why, Maria wondered suddenly, had she ever thought she could fit into Lonnie's world? This was where she belonged, in this ghetto of peeling paint and cracked concrete.

Maria ran until her sides ached. She didn't look back, but she could hear the snap-click of Lonnie's heels on the pavement behind her. "Stop, Maria," he called again.

She darted past the dimly lit Safeway store, closed early for New Year's Eve. Several people emerged from Palermo's Bar and Grill next door, laughing too brightly, their voices magnified by the cold, crystal silence of the night.

On impulse, Maria ducked past them into Palermo's and stood uncertainly in the gold-toned shadows. The atmosphere was heavy with cigarette smoke and the aromas of charbroiled burgers and deep-fried onions. The bar was decorated with holiday streamers, tinsel, and styrofoam bells. People milled about, calling New Year's greetings from one table to another, their voices blending in a garbled, monotonous din.

Maria felt self-conscious standing alone, a helpless waif beside the beeping, clanging video games. She stepped back toward the door, ready to run. Surely Lonnie had already gone on by. She turned and bumped hard against a solid, towering figure in a worn leather jacket. She looked up dazedly into the darkly sinister face of Raul Naranjo.

"Ah, Miss Fine Lady," he greeted slyly, taking her arm as if their encounter were prearranged. She jerked her arm free. He followed her outside and walked beside her, matching her hurried gait. "Aren't you gonna party for New Year's Eve?"

"I'm going home," she said.

"Not alone," he argued mockingly. "No one should be alone tonight."

She quickened her pace. "Please go away."

"No way, pretty baby. I told you once we'd talk again when it was just the two of us. Looks like that's now." He took her arm and led her forcibly down a narrow side street.

"This isn't the way home," she protested.

"It's *my* way home." He pulled her toward a dilapidated apartment building with a sagging porch and broken windows stuffed with cardboard. He put a possessive arm around her waist and directed her into a dreary, airless room with the barest of furnishings.

"Please—" she begged.

"I'm not gonna hurt you," he said, releasing her and holding his hands up, palms open. "I said we're just gonna talk, nice and private like. Get acquainted, you know?"

Maria cradled her arms against her chest. "Let me go, please." She could hardly hear her own voice over the terrified pounding of her heart.

Raul locked the door and dropped the key into his shirt pocket. "You go when I say." He nodded toward a dingy kitchenette. "You want some beer?"

"Water," she murmured. Was there another exit? While Raul occupied himself in the kitchenette, Maria stealthily opened the nearest door and slipped inside. She groaned, disappointed. No back door. And the only window was boarded shut. A single bare bulb glared from the tarnished ceiling fixture.

An obnoxious odor permeated the room. Ether. Maria wrinkled her nose in disgust. She walked cautiously over to an old-fashioned bathtub with molded feet next to a metal table brimming with chemical containers. Her eyes scanned the labels— sodium hydroxide, cyanide, hydrochloric acid. Plastic trash cans lined one wall. A narrow shelf contained an odd assortment of empty glass receptacles—amber vanilla extract bottles, salad oil cruets, baby bottles, and mayonnaise jars.

Suddenly, before Maria could move or utter a word, Raul was behind her, hovering over her. He yanked her out of the room and slammed the door. "OK, so now you know. This is a crack house. You tell anybody and you're dead meat."

"I won't," promised Maria, stepping back. "Just let me go home, please."

There was a cutting glint in Raul's eyes as he clasped her arm. "The party's just getting started, babe."

A knock sounded on Raul's door, followed by a familiar voice. "Hey, man, let me in." It was Enrique.

Raul angrily jabbed the key in the dead bolt lock and threw open the door. Enrique entered, his gaze darting from Maria to Raul, and demanded, "What's she doing here?"

"What's it to you?"

"I told you a long time ago, leave her alone!"

"What's the big deal? She your private property?"

"She's my friend. Let her go." Enrique looked at Maria. "Come on. Let's get out of here."

"Wait, man," said Raul. "We're buddies, right? Why not share a good thing?"

"You got a big mouth," growled Enrique.

"Your lady better keep *her* mouth shut about what she saw here or she's as good as dead."

"You touch her, man, and you're dead!" warned Enrique as he swept her past Raul down the weatherworn porch steps.

"How did you know I was here?" Maria stammered.

"I didn't," replied Enrique. "Raul and I had plans for to-night."

Maria stumbled on a jutting slab of sidewalk and caught Enrique's arm. "I can't stop trembling," she panted. "I was so scared."

"You won't make it home like this. My place is closer, OK?"

"No, I—I really shouldn't—"

"It's no problem. The place is quiet. Mama and the kids are at church tonight. Rita's off cheering up her friend Anna."

"Anna—the one who just had a baby? Is she sick?"

"No. She's crazy upset. The authorities stuck her baby in a foster home. Now Rita's scared they'll take her baby too when it's born."

"Why did they take Anna's baby?"

"They say he was born wacked out on cocaine."

Maria shuddered. It seemed that the whole world was out of joint tonight, messed up, hopeless. "Did you know Raul was making cocaine?" she asked as they entered Enrique's house.

Enrique flicked the light switch. "I told him he was loco. Everybody else took to the hills to brew that stuff, somewhere deserted, you know? The cops are gonna smell him out any day now."

Maria sat down on the lumpy sofa. She wanted to run straight home, but she couldn't let her grandmother see her like this. "I can't stop shaking," she said, hugging her arms.

"You sit back and relax. I've got something to help you." Enrique held out a narrow, twisted brown cigarette. "Blowing a little pot will take the edge off your nerves."

"I told you, I don't do drugs."

"Don't worry, it's not dusted. It's just grass." He sat down beside her. "Come on, I know you're no stoner, but a couple of puffs of this and you'll forget all your troubles."

"I wish I *could* forget," she murmured. She thought about her mother's death, her father's impending marriage, Lonnie's jealousy and mistrust, Lauren's cruelty, and Raul's vile threat on her life. If only she could ease the terrible pain and frustration she felt.

"Try it, Maria. One puff. You'll feel better, believe me."

"I can't, Enrique. I'm afraid . . . "

"Don't be, Maria. I like you. I wanna help you. I wouldn't let anything hurt you."

Maria pressed her knuckles against her lips. "How do I know pot won't hurt me?"

"Take one drag, that's all. If you don't like it, OK."

"Maybe just once," she relented, timidly taking the joint. Trembling, she placed the cigarette between her lips. It had a heavy, sweet, musty odor. She inhaled slowly, then more deeply, allowing the tendrils of smoke to fill her lungs. She coughed, disappointed. She didn't feel anything except a gagging reflex from the pungent smoke.

"Take another drag," said Enrique, lighting his own reefer.

She tried again. Several times. Her mouth felt dry. The room seemed brighter. Had Enrique turned on another light? Maria put her head back on the sofa and closed her eyes. There was something she was about to say. Something on her mind—a problem. It was elusive now. It didn't matter. Nothing mattered.

She felt mild and mellow. The whole world was yellow and bright and smooth, like the sun, like an egg, like a golden egg. She was curled inside the egg, cozy and warm and safe. Her pulse and heartbeat were moving in rhythm with the atmosphere; she was in tune with the universe. Nothing could reach her, touch her, disturb her. Her whole body purred with a delicious smoothness.

Across a great gulf she heard Enrique's voice. "Get up, Maria. Come on, we gotta move. Mama's home!"

She felt herself being hoisted up and nearly carried out the door. "I can walk," she protested, pushing Enrique away. How dare he intrude on her magical world, this golden-hued, free-floating fantasy she was enjoying!

Without Enrique's support, Maria's legs collapsed like string. He dragged her along the sidewalk like a rag doll. She recoiled against the cold air whipping her perspiring face. The night was too dark. What had happened to the brilliant lights?

Suddenly, from somewhere, Maria heard bells chiming and horns blasting. It had something to do with a new year, but the idea was vague, fleeting. What year? Who was celebrating?

Maria squinted through the darkness, groping for a familiar landmark, something solid and secure. Pangs of anxiety were swiftly replacing the warm, contented feelings. Where was she going? Who was taking her? What was happening?

Without warning, shadows loomed from every side like ghoulish phantoms. Her imagination summoned grotesque gargoyle heads that bobbed leeringly before her face. Maria's eyes teared; her heart beat accelerated, out of control. She clutched Enrique's arm. "It's like a roller coaster. I can't stop it. I can't hold on. Everything's going too fast."

"You're OK," he soothed. "You just took too much grass for the first time."

She gripped him with a desperation borne of abject panic. "Help me, please! I'm sick to my stomach. I can't think straight. Please don't let me go crazy. Don't let me die!"

15

Maria woke the next morning with a dull, pounding headache. She felt guilty, depressed. Why had she smoked marijuana, surrendering control of her mind to something or someone else, perhaps to the devil himself? She hadn't intended to. It just happened. Did that mean it could "just happen" again? Was that how drug addiction began? She shuddered as she recalled that paralyzing sensation of opening herself to evil, making herself vulnerable to what seemed now to have been wickedness personified.

She couldn't put it into words, couldn't even begin to explain her feelings, but this morning as she struggled to pray, she felt Jesus' Spirit cautioning her, convicting her. She remembered her pastor saying that a Christian's body was the house where the Holy Spirit lived. Had smoking pot actually opened the door of her mind-house to Satan?

Today, Maria felt distant from God, forlorn, far removed from the peace and joy that Jesus' presence usually gave her. She groped for the words to voice a prayer. Finally, in desperation, the plea welled from deep within her. "Forgive me, Jesus," she whispered. "I don't want anyone to control my mind but You. I want to please You. I love You, Jesus."

Maria had one last bit of unfinished business. She took paper and pencil and scribbled an anonymous note to the police, informing them that a crack house operated in her neighborhood. She didn't mention Raul's name or her own. She couldn't risk involving Grandma Estrella in this unsavory situation, nor did she wish to incur Raul's wrath. But at least the police would be on the alert, and sooner or later they would catch Raul Naranjo.

At ten that morning Lonnie telephoned Maria. "Thank God, you're home," he exclaimed. "You had me worried out of my mind, the way you ran off last night. I looked everywhere. Where'd you go?"

"I—I ran into a friend. He took me home."

"Well, I'm just glad you're OK. May I come over?" he asked, sounding contrite.

"We don't have anything to talk about," Maria said coolly.

"Yes, we do," said Lonnie. "I'll be there in an hour."

Maria was standing on her porch in her angora sweater and plaid dirndl skirt when Lonnie arrived. "I don't want Grandma Estrella to know about our fight," she told him.

"We could go to my house, but everyone's watching the parade."

"How about the park? We could sit on the swings."

Lonnie nodded. "Come on. I'll drive us."

The park was nearly deserted. Maria took one swing, Lonnie the one beside her. For several minutes they swung in silence.

Then Lonnie said, "We've got to talk about our misunderstanding. Were you really at the restaurant that night with your father?"

"Yes," Maria admitted resignedly. "I lied when I told you he was dead."

"Why?"

"I didn't mean to. I just didn't want you to know he had deserted me."

"That doesn't make any sense. Did you think I'd pity you or think badly of you?"

"I don't know. I just wanted to fit in like everyone else. I didn't want you to think I was different."

"But that's what I like about you, Maria. You *are* different. That's why I got so angry when I thought you were cheating on me, like Lauren would."

"I wasn't! I never would."

"I know that now." He reached over for her hand. "I'm sorry I accused you and blew up like I did."

"I'm sorry I lied about my father."

"Let's call it a fair exchange, OK?"

Maria nodded, smiling. They talked for another hour. Maria found herself telling Lonnie about her unshakable sense of loss over her mother's death and her father's absence, and about his unexpected plan to remarry.

Lonnie shared a secret of his own—the rough years he had experienced before his parents became Christians. "My father's a recovered alcoholic," he confessed. "He used to get violent and abusive with my mom and me. When I was a kid, fear was the only feeling I had for my dad."

Maria stared at Lonnie in astonishment. "I thought your parents were almost perfect."

"They're not perfect, but they're pretty terrific," said Lonnie. "My dad hasn't had a drink since he joined Alcoholics Anonymous. When he came to Jesus five years ago, our family really started pulling together." Lonnie glanced at his watch. "I'd better get you home so you can spend some of New Year's Day with your grandmother. And I promised my dad we'd watch the football game together."

They walked back to Lonnie's car hand in hand. "Let's promise never to fight again," he suggested. "And no more secrets between us, OK?"

Maria nodded half-heartedly. Her throat tightened. *I already have another secret,* she reflected with a stab of guilt. *What would Lonnie say if he knew I spent last evening smoking pot with Enrique Fernandez?*

In spite of Maria's drug-dazed, nightmare memory of New Year's Eve, she found the months of January and February to be happy and fulfilling. She and Lonnie were closer than they had ever been. Every weekend they sang together at a different church in the area. Their popularity spread by word of mouth until they found it necessary to turn down invitations.

Maria thrived on singing with Lonnie. Privately, she preferred performing at neighboring churches to attending her own. Lauren, Denise, and the other girls in their clique made it clear they didn't approve of her relationship with Lonnie. Whenever they caught Maria alone, they were catty and cruel, quick with put-downs and cutting remarks. Around Lonnie, they were all sweetness and honey. "We've missed you, Lonnie," Lauren would purr. "When are you coming back to us?" The shower of female attention always made Lonnie beam, but Lauren's syrupy, cloying tones turned Maria's stomach.

As the weeks of the new year slipped by, Maria avoided Enrique Fernandez. Finally, summoning her courage, she faced him squarely one evening and told him that under no circumstances could she permit a replay of New Year's Eve. Too much was at stake—her commitment to Christ, her relationship with her boyfriend Lonnie, and her own fragile, growing self-esteem. To her amazement, Enrique seemed genuinely touched. He accepted her words without argument.

At the same time, Maria's friendship with Enrique's sister flourished. As Rita's pregnancy advanced, she seemed more depressed, more in need of sympathy and reassurance. Maria found she liked feeling needed. Rita's sense of helplessness and dependency struck a responsive chord, reminding Maria of the painful, precious days she had spent as care-giver to her dying mother. Maria would have expected to shun such a familiar role, but she derived surprising satisfaction in nurturing and encouraging Rita.

One Sunday morning in early March, as Lonnie and Maria sang a duet in their own church, Enrique slipped into the sanctuary looking agitated and distressed. Maria stared at him, nearly forgetting the words she was singing. *Why would Enrique come here?* she wondered. What was wrong? After the duet, Enrique motioned furiously for her to come. When she reached him, he quickly ushered her out to the vestibule, ignoring the curious stares of the congregation. Lonnie followed and stood beside Maria with a protective hand on her shoulder. "Who are you?" he asked Enrique. "What do you want?"

Enrique gazed intently at Maria. "You must come with me," he told her breathlessly. "It's Rita. Her baby is coming. She wants you. Please, we must hurry."

Maria glanced helplessly from Enrique to Lonnie. "I can't, Enrique. I wouldn't know what to do for her."

"Just be there, Maria. Please, she needs you."

"She should go to the hospital, Enrique."

"No, she won't go. She's afraid, after what they did to Anna."

"But the doctors can give Rita the care she needs."

Enrique's expression hardened. "They would take away her baby like they did Anna's."

"But Anna took cocaine." Maria stared at him in alarm. "Are you saying Rita took cocaine too?"

Enrique clasped her arm urgently. "Please come, Maria."

Lonnie stepped between them. "Maria, what's this all about?"

"Enrique's sister is my friend. She's having a baby. She needs me."

"Don't go," said Lonnie firmly. "It's not your business, Maria. Let a doctor handle it."

Enrique's eyes darkened with disappointment. "Are you coming, Maria?"

"Yes," she replied, her gaze darting between the two opposing figures. She turned entreatingly to Lonnie. "I'm Latino . . . and a Christian. I've got to go with Enrique. Please understand."

Lonnie stepped back, his eyes narrowing with apprehension. "You can't go alone, Maria. Let me go with you."

"No, Lonnie. I'll be all right, I promise," she called as Enrique hurried her out the door.

When they reached Enrique's house, Maria could hear Rita screaming. "Enrique, your sister has to have a doctor," she told him. "If she won't go to the hospital, we've got to find someone who will deliver the baby here."

Enrique emitted a hard, mirthless laugh. "Who would come here?"

"Grandma Estrella's friend Mrs. Ramiriz used to be a midwife."

"I'll get her." As Enrique left for Mrs. Ramiriz, Maria tiptoed into the small, sunless bedroom where Rita lay doubled over in pain, moaning prayers in Spanish. Her eyes were dark and beseeching as she stretched a limp hand toward Maria. Maria went to her and stroked her moist forehead.

"It'll be OK, Rita," she murmured, trying to sound convincing.

Rita was tearful. "The baby's not due till next month. What if something is wrong? What if my baby dies?"

"Let me call the paramedics, Rita," coaxed Maria. "They'll take you to the hospital. The doctors will know what to do."

"No! If they find crack in my baby, they'll put him in a foster home," Rita wailed.

Maria shook her head in dismay. "Why did you take cocaine, Rita? Didn't you know it could hurt your baby?"

"I took crack and speed and ice before I knew about the baby. Then I figured it was too late. More crack wouldn't matter." Rita winced and stiffened. "The pains are getting worse, Maria. Call my mama at work."

Maria ran to the living room just as Enrique entered with Mrs. Ramiriz. "Thank you for coming," Maria cried, embracing her.

"Is many years since I bring babies into world," said the sturdy old woman. "You help me, yes?"

Maria swallowed hard. "I—I can boil water, I guess—"

"You get clean sheets. Make place to put the baby."

Rita's mother arrived home shortly after noon and took Maria's place at Rita's bedside. Even as Maria busied herself in the living room with the younger boys, she could hear Rita's long, agonizing cries from the bedroom. As evening approached, Maria fixed chicken enchiladas and served them to Enrique and his brothers. She took plates to Mrs. Ramiriz and Rita's mother. "There's hot coffee and Jell-O if Rita feels like eating anything," she whispered.

Mrs. Fernandez shook her head. "She is finally dozing, Maria. She is so tired, but I think the baby will come soon now."

Shortly after 8:00 P.M. Maria heard a strangled, high-pitched cry from the bedroom. Rita's baby! Several minutes later, Mrs. Ramiriz brought out a squirming bundle in Grandma Estrella's handmade quilt. "Is a boy," she announced, rocking the baby gently.

"He's so little," exclaimed Maria as she folded back the corners of the blanket to peer at the tiny, squashed, red face.

"He have trouble breathing," said Mrs. Ramiriz as she placed the baby in Maria's arms. "You watch him very close while we take care of his mama."

Maria sat down on the sofa and cradled the infant while Enrique's brothers crowded around in amazement. "He's funny-looking," said five-year-old José.

"All newborn babies look funny," explained Maria. But the idea bothered her. There was something about Rita's baby that appeared not quite right. His eyes held an odd, trancelike stare. His body would grow rigid; then he would shiver and lapse into a weak, whining cry.

The baby remained jittery and inconsolable, gasping for breath one minute and emitting a shrill, distressed sob the next. Maria nervously paced the floor with him, praying silently. She sighed with relief when Mrs. Fernandez finally took the baby in to Rita to nurse. Maybe now he would calm down and be content. But before long, Rita's mother was back, rocking the baby in her arms, frantically trying to soothe him. "He won't nurse," she told Maria wearily. "He's irritable and unhappy."

"Maybe all new babies are that way," offered Maria.

"Not my six babies," replied Mrs. Fernandez. "My babies were big and healthy and hungry. But this baby . . . " She shook her head sadly and turned away before Maria could see her expression.

16

The telephone jangled early Saturday morning just as Maria returned from a disturbing visit to Rita and her fretful little baby, Roberto. Maria murmured a distracted hello into the receiver, then brightened as she recognized Sarah's voice. She sounded so excited Maria could barely comprehend her words. "Slow down, Sarah. Tell me again . . . slowly."

"It's happened," Sarah gasped. "Brett and I—we're going steady! He asked me last night."

"That's totally neat. You two were meant for each other."

Sarah laughed. "I wasn't sure Brett would ever have eyes for anything besides computer chips."

"Tell me every detail," enthused Maria. "What did he say? How did he sound?"

"Oh, I'll play the whole thing for you when I see you."

"Play the whole thing?"

"Yeah, it's all on tape—every crazy, wonderful, romantic word."

"You recorded your evening with Brett? Isn't that a little weird?"

"Oh, no, I didn't tape it," corrected Sarah. "My darling little brothers did it. They planted their recorder behind the sofa. I woke up this morning hearing Brett's voice booming in the back yard. The twins had all their friends over listening. Even charged them a nickel apiece. It was the most ghastly experience of my life. My whole neighborhood heard Brett telling me I was more important to him than all the computer software in the world.''

"Oh, Sarah, how could they? What did you do?''

"I confiscated all their video game cartridges until they turned the tape over to me. At first I was mad enough to strangle them. But now l'm sort of glad I can replay Brett's words whenever I please. Who knows when he'll ever be so romantic again?''

"You'd better keep the tape out of the wrong hands,'' giggled Maria, "or it could end up number one on the charts.''

"Oh, poor Brett would simply fade into a micro-processor!''

"When do I get to hear this romantic masterpiece?''

"Sooner than you think. Brett is actually driving me to the DMV today to get my driver's license. If I survive the test, he'll let me borrow his Mustang.''

"He really must be in love,'' teased Maria.

"Just don't tell him about the tape,'' cautioned Sarah. "If all goes well, I'll see you tonight. Be ready for the ride of your life.''

Sarah arrived at Maria's at six, her freckled face glowing as she stepped out of Brett's shiny automobile. "I did it! I passed!''

"I'm impressed,'' said Maria.

"Hop in . . . unless you're afraid.''

"Afraid?'' echoed Maria, promptly climbing in. "Sarah, you know I'd trust you with my life.''

"Let's hope it doesn't come to that.''

"Where are we going?'' Maria asked as she buckled her seat belt.

"To Denise Vanderwall's.''

"Denise?'' Maria wrinkled her nose.

"I know,'' said Sarah, pulling out into the street. "She's Lauren's best friend. But she's also in charge of the beach party the youth group is planning for April first.''

"Oh, I heard about that,'' mused Maria. "It's 'The Big Beach Bash to Welcome Spring with a Splash!' ''

"That's Lauren's creative genius. Actually, the party's going to be a fabulous luau. Everyone's into it.''

"I didn't know. Lonnie and I have been away singing so much lately."

"You are going, aren't you?"

"I don't know, Sarah. I don't know how to swim . . . and to tell you the truth, I'm petrified of the water."

"You don't have to swim. There'll be plenty to do, and Lonnie will keep you busy. Besides, I'm head of the decorating committee," continued Sarah. "I was hoping you'd help me out."

"I guess so, but what's that got to do with Denise?"

"She has loads of Hawaiian decorations she promised to lend me. You know, her parents practically live in the Islands."

"So I've heard. Must be nice."

"I'm not so sure. Imagine never having your folks around."

Maria stared somberly out the window. "I know."

Sarah gave her a horrified glance. "I'm sorry, Maria. I didn't mean—"

"It's OK. I'm getting used to living my life without parents."

"You're just saying that."

"Yeah, but who knows? Maybe someday I'll believe it."

Sarah merged haltingly with the early evening traffic. "I'm not taking the freeway. These surface streets are bad enough."

"You're braver than I am," said Maria.

Sarah smiled. "I just want to see Denise's face when I drive up in Brett's Mustang."

A half hour later Sarah pulled to a stop before a luxurious condominium in Hacienda Heights.

"Does Denise know we're coming?" asked Maria.

"No. She said she'd bring the leis, lanterns, and stuff to church tomorrow, but I know she won't remember. She's such a scatterbrain."

Sarah and Maria gazed admiringly at the sprawling, white-trimmed stucco building with its private sundecks, balconies and greenhouse windows. "I could get used to living like this," confided Sarah with a grin as they approached the patio entry. "How about you, Maria?"

"Not if it meant sharing a room with Denise Vanderwall."

Sarah knocked on the door. When no one answered, she knocked again. "Someone's home. I hear music playing."

"It must be Denise. Her parents wouldn't play heavy metal."

The door opened finally, and Denise swayed toward them, smiling dreamily, her round face framed by an untidy mane of red hair. "Sarah, Maria," she cooed. "How nice. You came to my party."

"Party? I just stopped by for the decorations for the luau."

"Come in," said Denise, leading them through a ceramic-tiled entrance way into an ornate room with skylights, vaulted ceiling, and a massive stone fireplace. Looking around, Maria spotted several familiar faces from school and church . . . including Lauren's.

"We didn't know you were having a party," Maria told Denise as Lauren strolled over in her usual lofty manner.

Surprisingly, Lauren offered a smile instead of a cutting remark. "Sarah, Maria, hello! Isn't it a wonderful, incredible night!"

Maria forced a wary smile. She couldn't think of a thing to say, but Lauren didn't give her a chance anyway. "You know, Maria, I've never told you this before, but when you sing, you sound like a nightingale. I suppose that sounds preposterous coming from me, but that's what my mother says about you. She's one of your greatest fans." She paused. "Do you have any idea how a nightingale sounds?"

"No, I—" Maria began, but Lauren cut her off.

"I think it must be beautiful, the most beautiful sound on earth. Sometimes I think I could sound that way. I could have a voice like yours. No one has really given me a chance, have they? No one has ever really listened to me sing. Have you, Maria? Have you heard me?"

"I—I don't remember," stammered Maria.

"See what I mean? I could be missing the chance of my life simply because I haven't sung for anyone. I could be singing with Lonnie, performing before huge crowds, receiving their praises just like you." She clasped Maria's arm confidentially. "Look what singing has done for you, Maria. Changed you from a shabby, shy little mouse into—"

Maria pulled away from Lauren and looked helplessly at Sarah. "Is she drunk? What's going on here?"

"I'm afraid to find out," said Sarah, glancing around. Several classmates lolled about on sofas and chairs, looking dazed, disoriented. The room vibrated with the pounding, brassy beat of hard rock.

"Where are your parents?" Maria asked Denise.

"Out of town," she shrugged. "They told me to have fun, so I am."

"Well, we just stopped by for the Hawaiian decorations for the beach party," Sarah shouted as the electronic sounds crescendoed.

Denise turned down the stereo, then motioned Sarah and Maria over to a large oak table. Maria stared in stunned dismay at the glass water pipes, measuring spoons, mirrors and a bottle of rum. Beside a cellophane packet of white powder lay an assortment of rock-like crystals.

"Help yourself. We've got it all—crack and ice," Denise said casually.

"Oh, no, cocaine," Maria said under her breath. "And speed."

"It's sure not sugar," replied Sarah.

"Have you ever snorted coke?" Denise asked them. "Here's all you do." She tapped the fine powder onto a hand mirror, lining it up in neat little rows, then held it to her nose and sniffed the dust into her nostrils. She closed her eyes and inhaled deeply. "Oh, wow, what energy, what warmth! Try it, Maria. Try it."

Maria shrank back. "No thanks! We've really got to go, Denise. If you'd just get the decorations."

Denise smiled vaguely. "They're in my mother's closet. I'll be right back."

A tall, muscular guy in designer sport shirt and jeans approached the table, took out a cigarette lighter, and heated a glass pipe filled with rum and cocaine. When his gaze met Maria's, he remarked, "Free base coke—it's pure, potent. Sends you right to the sky, soaring, man." He chuckled. "Or if you want a high that'll last all night, try a hit of ice! It's totally radical!"

"Get a life, buddy," snapped Sarah.

Sarah and Maria moved quickly from the table back to the front door. "I just hope the police don't raid this place before we get out of here," Sarah murmured.

"Let's go now," urged Maria.

"Not until I get those decorations. I drove too far to go home empty-handed."

"If Denise had her way, we'd go home stoned out of our minds."

They waited ten minutes. Then Sarah went looking for Denise. While Maria stood alone, fidgeting impatiently, Lauren sauntered over with an icy stare. "You still here, Maria?"

"We're going soon," Maria replied. She noted that the rosy flush in Lauren's face was gone. Lauren looked suddenly haggard, spent.

"I know what you're going to do, Maria." Lauren rubbed her slender fingers together nervously. "You're going straight to Lonnie, aren't you?"

"Go to Lonnie?"

"You're going to tell him I sniffed coke. You think that'll keep us apart, but it won't. It's just a matter of time before Lonnie's mine again."

"Lauren, you should go home." Maria touched her arm lightly. "Sarah could drive you."

Lauren irritably jerked her arm away. "I'm staying right here. I just need more coke."

"Don't, Lauren."

"Why not, Maria?" Lauren's lavender-shadowed eyes narrowed. "Can you honestly tell me you've never done drugs?"

Maria turned away, shaken. Lauren pursued her with a barrage of accusations. "I know about you, Maria. I checked out that guy who came looking for you that morning in church. Enrique Fernandez, a friend of drug pushers, maybe an addict himself. Has he turned you on to drugs, Maria? Does Lonnie know?"

Maria shook her head in protest. "Lauren, no, please—"

"I was wrong about the man in the restaurant," Lauren continued, growing increasingly agitated, "but I'm not wrong now. I can see it in your eyes. You've tried drugs. When the time's right, Maria, I'm going to tell Lonnie all about you. Then we'll see which one of us he chooses."

"How can you condemn Enrique or me when you're high on cocaine?" countered Maria.

"I'm no drug addict," snapped Lauren. "Coke just gives me a lift—boosts my confidence, makes me feel good."

Maria studied Lauren for a moment. "I don't understand," she said. "You have everything a person could ask for—loving parents, friends, money. You're beautiful and popular. Why would you need to get stoned?"

Lauren looked away, her expression sullen. "Don't kid yourself, Maria. I don't have everything. No one has everything."

On the drive home, neither Maria nor Sarah spoke for a while. Maria noticed Sarah's hands trembling on the steering wheel. Her own hands were shaking too, so she kept them clutched tightly in her lap. Finally, Sarah pulled into the parking lot of a frozen yogurt shop.

"Are you hungry?" Maria asked in surprise.

"No," said Sarah thickly, "I feel like throwing up. I just had to stop driving and calm down. Look, my hands are shaking!"

"I know. You're upset about what happened at Denise's."

"Aren't you?" countered Sarah. "I always suspected. I mean, you hear things at school—about kids doing drugs. But these kids are from our own youth group, Maria. They're Christian kids! How can they do it like it's no big deal?"

"I don't know," murmured Maria. She didn't want to get into this with Sarah. Not after Lauren had just reminded her of her own pot-smoking escapade with Enrique. She was no better than Lauren and Denise. How could she condemn them?

"Are you listening to me, Maria?" demanded Sarah. "I was saying, aren't you upset too? What are we going to do?"

"Do?"

"We should tell someone. They need help—Lauren and Denise and the others. They could kill themselves, Maria. You read about it all the time—someone overdosing, or going crazy, or *dying!*"

101

"Who could we tell? They'd hate us. Who would believe us?"

Sarah hit her palm against the steering wheel. "We can't just sit back and do nothing. That's what too many people do. Did you see that TV news program, where they said one out of every hundred Americans is a regular cocaine user? We can't just pretend it's not happening, Maria. Not when it's in our own backyard."

Maria bit her lower lip, searching for the right words. She wanted to help Lauren and the others, but she had to protect herself too. "If we get Lauren and Denise in trouble, maybe they'll lie about us. Maybe they'll say we were doing drugs too."

Sarah drew in a deep breath. "Well, we know the truth, don't we, Maria, and the truth always wins out."

That's what I'm afraid of, Maria reflected silently. She felt like a traitor, remembering how easily Enrique had convinced her to try pot.

Sarah shifted the Mustang into drive. "I know what we can do, Maria. We can talk to Michael Dodd. If anyone has the answers, it should be our youth director. You'll go with me, won't you? Maybe we can corner him after the beach bash, OK?"

When Maria didn't reply, Sarah rushed on urgently, "I'm so totally glad we're friends, Maria. I'm so glad you're not like Lauren and Denise. We're in this together, a fight to the finish. We'll take a stand and make a difference in our youth group. I just know God had it planned for us to find out about the drugs so we could do something to help Lauren and Denise and . . . "

Maria stared out the car window and shut her ears to Sarah's endless chatter. She wanted to stuff a sock in Sarah's mouth and tell her she was a dope to think Maria was so Snow White pure. But no! Sarah—and Lonnie!—must never find out that Maria had behaved like a common druggie, that she was just as guilty as Lauren and Denise and their crack-snorting friends.

17

Hey, Maria," Lonnie greeted, "are you ready for the big beach bash to welcome spring with a splash?" He stood at the door in his Hawaiian print shirt and cutoff jeans, his tanned face glowing with energy and excitement.

Maria motioned him inside. "You're early. Let me get my beach towel and picnic basket."

"Don't forget your swimsuit."

"I'm wearing it under my shorts and blouse. But don't count on me for much swimming."

"Why not? Don't imported Coloradans take to the water?"

"Not if they can't swim."

"You're kidding."

"I wish I were." She shrugged helplessly. "What can I say? I'm scared to death of the water."

Lonnie gave her an impetuous hug. "I'll teach you, Maria. In no time I'll have you swimming circles around everyone else."

"I think I'd rather sunbathe on a safe, solid beach."

Grandma Estrella hobbled into the room, smiling, her arms wrapped around a large wicker basket. "Here is food, Maria, enough for many hungry people."

"Let me help you with that, Mrs. Estrella." Lonnie took the basket, giving the elderly woman a quick kiss on the forehead. "I bet you worked since dawn on all this chow."

Grandma Estrella waved him off with, "Maria don't let me work hard no more."

"But you do anyway," scolded Maria with an appreciative embrace. "You are my wonderful *Abuelita*."

Grandma Estrella's eyes moistened. "You, Maria, are beautiful light in my life."

Lonnie cleared his throat. "I hate to break up this mutual admiration society, but if Maria and I don't get going, we'll miss the beach party."

In the car on the way to Santa Monica Beach, Lonnie drew Maria close and said, "I'm really looking forward to being with you today."

"Me too," she said.

They were silent for several minutes as Lonnie settled into an even speed on the freeway. After a while he noted, "You seem quiet today, Maria. Is something on your mind?"

More than I can tell you about, Maria reflected somberly. Aloud she said, "There are a couple of things, Lonnie. My father called last night."

"Is everything OK?"

"Papa has set his wedding date for the end of June. I talked to Angela, the lady he's marrying. We've talked several times before, and she seems real nice. She asked me to be in the wedding."

"How do you feel about that?"

"I don't know. At first I was so angry about Papa remarrying. I didn't want him to replace Mama. But I know he's lonely. I remember how alone I felt when Papa brought me here to California. Now I have you and Sarah and my grandmother. And I have Jesus. Papa didn't have anyone until he met Angela."

"It sounds like you're accepting his remarriage."

"I'm trying to. I do want him to be happy."

"So you'll be visiting Colorado this summer?"

"I guess so." Maria gave Lonnie a sidelong glance. "Angela wants me to come live with Papa and her . . . permanently."

"Permanently? In Colorado? But your life is here, Maria. You aren't going, are you?"

"I don't know, Lonnie. I don't want to leave you. And Grandma Estrella needs me."

"Don't make any quick decisions. There are a lot of people here who care about you." He squeezed her shoulder. "I'm first on the list."

Maria could feel a smile, like a tickle inside her, going all the way to her toes. But a dark question followed, hovering ominously. *Would Lonnie still care as much if he knew about me smoking marijuana with Enrique Fernandez?*

Thinking of Enrique, Maria said, "There's something else I wanted to tell you." She hesitated. "Do you remember the boy who came looking for me in church?"

Lonnie nodded. "You befriended his sister. She was having a baby. Frankly, I had my doubts about you going off with that guy."

"Enrique has been very kind to me, Lonnie, and—well, my grandmother and I sort of invited him to the beach party."

Lonnie gave her a quick look. "How did that happen?"

"He was over fixing a broken porch step. He was feeling real down because this friend of his, Raul, got busted. Grandma Estrella told him he should go to church sometime and make friends with some decent kids. Then she mentioned the beach party. Enrique laughed it off, but I told him he should come. Lonnie, he needs to know about Jesus. I'm not very good at telling him, so I figured . . . "

Lonnie smiled. "You figured you'd let our youth director do it."

"Enrique's never been to the ocean," continued Maria. "No one in his family has. Grandma Estrella says that's how it is for most of the people in our neighborhood. They get in a rut and can never get out. They're afraid even to cross gang territory to go anywhere."

"It sounds depressing," mused Lonnie. "You haven't said. Is Enrique coming today?"

"He just might show up. He's got his friend Raul's car. He said if he can get it working, he'll be there."

"Do you think he'll feel at home in our group?"

Maria looked appraisingly at Lonnie. "I guess it's up to us to make him feel at home."

"You've got a point," conceded Lonnie. "Let's hope everyone else looks at it that way." He took the next off ramp and headed for the beach cities. "I hope this sunshine holds," he told Maria. "I've been waiting all winter to get back to the sand and surf."

Maria smiled vaguely. "It should be fun," she murmured, but her thoughts were still on Enrique. If she really wanted Enrique to feel at home, she should have invited him to ride with Lonnie and her. But she had wanted this time alone with Lonnie.

Just before ten, Lonnie pulled into the beach parking lot. As he helped Maria from the car, she stared in mute fascination at the endless expanse of ocean. The morning sun shimmered on the water, casting a crystal sheen. The white-capped waves glistened like diamonds as they surged over the sand and retreated in a rhythmic ballet. The whole world gleamed with an eye-blinding intensity.

"You haven't seen the ocean either, have you, Maria?"

"Not since I was a child," she murmured. "It's incredible."

Lonnie hoisted their gear onto his shoulder and took Maria's hand. "Everyone should be over at the pavilion," he told her. "Come on. Take off your sandals, and we'll run barefoot through the sand."

They met Brett and Sarah on their way. "The gang's all here," said Sarah, looking breezy in a neon print camp shirt and denim shorts, her freckles already toasty brown. "We saved a table for you two. And I brought gobs of marshmallows to roast over the bonfire tonight. This party should be awesome."

Brett pushed his glasses up on his nose and confided, "Sarah's already agreed I can bury her in the sand."

"I said no such thing," she protested. "I told you we could build a sand castle with moats and turrets and dragons and fair maidens all around."

"Well, here's the fair maiden," said Lonnie, lifting Maria's hand.

"And here's the dragon," laughed Sarah as she clasped Brett's arm.

"What are we waiting for?" exclaimed Maria. "Let's build a castle!"

After an hour of castle building, Lonnie and Maria joined the beach races, running in the brisk, salty air. They had water fights in the foaming surf and sunbathed under the hot noontime sun.

"Chow's on!" someone called shortly after one. Lonnie and Maria brushed the sticky coating of sand from their arms and legs and shook out their beach towels. "Last one to the pavilion gets dunked in the ocean!" teased Lonnie, darting ahead.

"Not fair!" cried Maria. "You're too big to dunk!"

As they took their seats at the long wooden picnic table, Lauren approached in a scanty bikini and net overblouse. She set a Hawaiian fruit salad on the table, then said confidentially to Maria, "You and Lonnie look so cozy together. Maybe I should have my little talk with him today."

"Why don't you just leave us alone?" said Maria curtly.

"You think I won't tell him about you trying drugs, don't you? But what do I have to lose?"

"I could tell him about you taking cocaine," argued Maria.

"It would be your word against mine, and Denise would deny it ever happened." Lauren smiled smugly, then strolled over to Lonnie and slipped her arm into his. "We haven't talked in ages, honey," she murmured, "and do I have a secret to share with you!"

"You'll have to take a number, Lauren," said Lonnie. He reached over for Maria's hand. "My days are booked, as you can see."

"Too bad," said Lauren peevishly. "But I'll catch you sooner or later, Lonnie." She sashayed away, making the most of every move.

Maria wasn't hungry anymore. Her throat tightened with apprehension, but her dark reverie was broken when Sarah nudged her. "Forget Lauren, Maria. Look who's here." She nodded toward a lone figure in faded T-shirt and jeans sauntering toward the pavilion.

"Enrique," gasped Maria. She didn't need him here now to complicate matters. Reluctantly she slipped from her seat, greeted Enrique, and made perfunctory introductions. "Everyone, this is my neighbor Enrique Fernandez. Enrique, you've met

Lonnie and Sarah. And that's Michael Dodd, our youth director. Next to him are Brett, Lauren, and—''

Enrique was obviously ill at ease. He endured the introductions with one-syllable grunts and nods. Maria could feel the curious stares of her companions and read their silent questions. *Who is this strange barrio guy? What is he doing here?* Lauren ambled over and whispered mockingly, ''You made it real easy for me, Maria. Just make sure he doesn't try to sell Lonnie a joint.''

''Take a long walk off a short pier, Lauren,'' snapped Maria.

''Give me one minute alone with Lonnie. That's all I need.''

Maria pivoted sharply. ''Come sit at my table, Enrique, with Lonnie and me.''

Enrique sat down opposite Maria and stretched out his lanky legs. ''Man, that ocean out there is unreal. I wish Rita could see it.''

''You should have brought her,'' said Maria, handing him a platter of barbecued chicken.

He speared several pieces. ''Rita's stuck with that squalling baby. He cries day and night. Rita's climbing the walls with him. I don't know who cries more, him or her.''

''I've told her I'd babysit sometime so she could get out.''

''That baby's too much for anyone to handle,'' muttered Enrique. ''He's just not what Rita expected. The whole thing's a real bummer.''

''I'm sorry,'' said Maria. ''I know how much Rita wanted someone to take away her loneliness.''

''That baby sure won't do it. He's driving us all loco.''

They lapsed into an uneasy silence, except for Lonnie's occasional stabs at conversation. ''You go to school, Enrique?''

''I dropped out in eighth grade.''

''You work then?''

''Laid off.''

''You got plans for the future?''

''Staying alive.''

After lunch, Maria, Lonnie, and Enrique walked along the beach and waded in the surf. ''How about a swimming lesson?'' suggested Lonnie.

"After all that food I'd sink like an anchor," said Maria. She didn't want to admit that the water terrified her.

Lonnie pulled her toward him, then looked over at Enrique. "I promised I'd teach her to swim like a fish. Wanna join us?"

Enrique waved him off. "I'll watch, man."

"Suit yourself. Come on, Maria. The others are already out there having a ball."

With growing anxiety Maria allowed Lonnie to lead her out into the water. Salt spray stung her eyes and left an acrid taste in her mouth. The unrelenting waves lapped against her, pushing, pulling, back and forth. As she struggled to keep her balance, the sand gave way beneath her feet. She clutched Lonnie in terror.

"I've got you, Maria. I'm going to teach you how to float."

"Take me back, Lonnie. Please!"

"Take it easy, Maria. Your fingernails are digging into my arms."

"Lonnie, I'm scared!"

"There's nothing to it. You just lie back, and my arms will keep you from sinking."

Before Maria could utter another protest, someone screamed. Lauren. She was farther out than Lonnie and Maria. Her arms frantically flailed the water. "Help, Lonnie! Got leg cramp—can't—" Her words were severed by the surging tide.

"Stay here, Maria," instructed Lonnie. "You'll be OK. I've got to help Lauren." He dove into the spumy whitecaps and swam away with strong, swift strokes.

"Wait, Lonnie," cried Maria. "Don't leave me alone!" She moved toward him in blind panic and faltered, caught in the under-current. The rising swell heaved over her. She gulped sea water, choking. The bitter, briny liquid shot up her nostrils and gushed down her throat in a caustic deluge. She couldn't breathe. There was suddenly no up or down, no air above or sand below. Only water, swirling around her, invading her sinuses, filling her lungs.

Then, after what seemed forever, strong arms wrapped around her and lifted her up. "Don't fight me, Maria. I'm no swimmer either." Enrique's voice. Holding her like a child against his chest, he slogged through the rolling water back to shore. He laid her on the wet, packed sand and dropped down beside her, his breath coming in quick gasps. Maria coughed, sputtered, and vomited sea water. As her mind cleared, she became aware of a crowd gathering around her.

"Are you OK, Maria?" cried Sarah, wrapping a beach towel around her.

"She almost drowned," someone exclaimed.

"The new guy saved her," said someone else.

Then Lonnie stooped down beside her, taking her hands in his. "Maria, are you all right? I'm so sorry I left you alone."

Maria tried to force words from her throat, but water bubbled out instead. She looked up and saw Lauren standing near Lonnie.

Lonnie looked up too and said accusingly, "When I reached you, Lauren, you weren't drowning. What's the idea, pulling a stunt like that?"

"I just wanted to spend a few minutes alone with you, Lonnie," Lauren said haughtily. "How'd I know Maria couldn't swim?"

"Your selfishness could have cost Maria her life," charged Sarah. "How could you be so cruel?"

Denise stepped forward beside Lauren. "Come off it, Sarah. Maria's no little angel like Lonnie thinks. Tell them, Lauren."

"It's true, Lonnie," Lauren asserted. "Maria's not the sweet, innocent girl you think she is."

"Knock it off, Lauren," Lonnie demanded.

"Maria hates drugs as much as I do," declared Sarah indignantly.

"Oh, really? I heard she's done drugs with her friend here, this Enrique Fernandez character," persisted Lauren. "He runs with drug pushers. He may even be one himself, for all we know. Think about it, Lonnie. Is Maria really the sort of girl you want?"

"Stop lying, Lauren," ordered Lonnie. "Tell her, Maria."

Lauren smiled smugly. "She can't call me a liar, Lonnie, because she knows what I've said is true. Isn't it, Maria?"

"It's forgiven, Lauren," Maria wept. "Why won't you let me forget?"

Enrique leaned forward, still breathing hard from his rescue effort, his eyes shadowed with anger and distrust. "Hey, dudes, I'm outta here!" He stood up and pulled his wet T-shirt over his head, then took the towel Sarah offered and dried his face and hair. "I don't know what's going on here," he said, tossing the towel back to Sarah. "I came here today because Maria thinks you got something I ain't found in drugs."

"We've got plenty," someone hooted. "What's the matter? Aren't we good enough for you Chicanos?"

"Where I come from, everybody's out for himself," uttered Enrique rawly. "You figure you better kill your enemy or he'll come back and kill you. You stake out your own turf and stay clear of where you don't belong. You got nobody but yourself, and when your number's up, ain't nothing you can do to change it." His stormy eyes probed one person, then another, before he looked down sadly at Maria and said, "Looks to me like your friends got life figured out about the same as me. 'Watch out for number one!'"

18

Before Maria realized what was happening, pandemonium broke out. Everyone was talking, arguing, swiftly drawing sides. *What about Maria? Is Lauren lying? What happened? Are Lauren and Maria fighting over Lonnie? How is that stranger involved?* Shouts of protest and angry accusations rose in the air— Lonnie scolding Lauren, Denise rushing to Lauren's defense, Sarah speaking up for Maria. Lauren quickly assumed the attack: "See what happens when we let low-riders into our group?"

Michael Dodd, the youth director, urgently attempted to restore calm, but no one could hear him above the din.

Maria sat shivering, wrapped in her beach towel, too humiliated to speak. Enrique helped her stand. Her legs were still weak, unsteady. "Let's get out of here," he whispered.

Maria nodded. Amid the commotion, they slipped away.

"You do not belong with those gringos," Enrique told her as he headed Raul's chugalug Chevy toward the nearest freeway onramp. "Why do you go to their fancy church, Maria? We have our own barrio churches."

Maria fought back sudden tears. "Because that's where I learned about Jesus, about Him being a real Person who could be my Savior and Friend. Jesus isn't like them, Enrique. He really loves me. He accepts me just as I am."

Enrique laughed skeptically. "No one does that, Maria."

"Jesus does," she insisted. "You've got to know Him to know what His love is like, Enrique. He even died to save me."

Enrique's mouth twisted. "Well, no one would ever die for me."

"But Jesus did die for you, Enrique. That's what I wanted you to find out today. I didn't know how to tell you. I wanted you to see Jesus' love in my friends."

"Yeah, I saw what they thought of me, Maria. It didn't have nothing to do with Jesus or love."

By late afternoon Enrique pulled his wheezing automobile to a stop beside his small, weathered house. "Can you come in a minute and see Rita?" he asked Maria. "I know you're feeling down right now, but she could use some cheering, too."

"I'll try," said Maria half-heartedly, climbing out of the car.

Even before Enrique opened the front door, Maria heard Rita's baby screaming. She and Enrique rushed in and found the bawling infant lying in the middle of the living room floor, kicking frantically, his tiny face red and pinched with distress.

Rita sat sprawled in the corner, rocking back and forth, her eyes white, her tongue protruding as she banged her head against the wall. She was drooling and crying.

Maria drew back instinctively. "Oh, Rita, no!"

Enrique uttered a small, guttural exclamation as he strode past Maria to his sister. He hoisted her up in his arms and shook her. "Rita, what did you take? Come on, talk to me, baby!" He looked in desperation at Maria. "She's moonwalking, wacked out on crack or ice or angel dust. Who knows what she took? Is the baby OK?"

Maria gathered the frantic infant into her arms. "He looks funny, sick."

"She probably gave him something too," Enrique said angrily.

Without warning, Rita twisted out of Enrique's grasp and backed against the wall, her arms outstretched, tensed, her fingers splayed. "Don't touch me," she cried. "I hear you—I hear all of you! Leave me alone! You want me to die!"

"Rita, honey, it's me, Enrique."

"No, it's the voices. They won't stop. They want me to hurt Roberto . . . make him stop crying."

"No, Rita. It's the drugs. You promised not to take any more."

"I had to, Enrique," she moaned, clutching his T-shirt. "I was feeling bad. Real bad."

"But look at you now," he retorted. "You're a mess!"

"I just had a few hits off a joint." Rita wept uncontrollably. "The voices—they tell me to hurt Roberto . . . throw him outside. Leave him in the street. They kill me if I don't. Don't let them kill me, Enrique!"

"No one's going to hurt you, Rita. You need help."

"No! Stay back! I know you," she shrieked. "You're the devil. Don't touch me!" Rita began to tremble convulsively. She stared in trancelike terror at the walls and ceiling. "You let the bugs in, the spiders! Stop them! They're crawling on me!" She writhed to the floor, plucking at imaginary insects.

Enrique knelt beside her and seized her wrists. With startling energy, Rita shoved him backward across the room. From his crumpled position, Enrique looked up at Maria, dazed. "Get Roberto out of here," he ordered. "Call the paramedics. Hurry!"

Minutes later, three white-garbed attendants strapped an inconsolable Rita into a straitjacket. As they placed her on the stretcher, Maria telephoned Grandma Estrella and told her what had happened. "Enrique and I are going to the hospital with Rita," she said, her voice tremulous. "We want them to check baby Roberto too."

"Maria, your friends are here," said Grandma Estrella. "They look for you."

"What friends?"

"Lonnie and Sarah and Brett. They here now, want to see you."

"I can't see them, Grandmother. Enrique and I are following the ambulance to Los Angeles County-USC Medical Center."

Lonnie came on the line and said, "What's going on, Maria?"

Falteringly she told him about Rita. "It's terrible, Lonnie. I've got to go. The ambulance is pulling away."

"We'll meet you at the hospital," Lonnie promised. "Sarah and Brett say they're coming too."

"Hurry, Lonnie," cried Maria.

Except for baby Roberto's plaintive cries, the drive to the hospital was marked by an oppressive silence. Enrique was tense, his body rigid as he gripped the steering wheel. He murmured something in Spanish under his breath. *A prayer?* wondered Maria.

He tailgated the car in front of him. "Hurry up, man. I wanna see my sister before they lock her away somewhere." His voice caught with emotion. "She'll be scared without me. She don't know them."

"The doctors will help her, Enrique," said Maria. "They'll be kind to her."

Enrique rubbed his nose with the back of his hand. "You think she'll let them be kind? I seen guys trip out on angel dust. They're like animals. They chew bark off trees, walk through windows, even try to saw off their own arms. How can you be kind to someone that strong, ready to kill you?"

Enrique pulled up to the emergency entrance just as the paraamedics removed Rita from the ambulance and strapped her to a gurney. She screamed and twisted, thrashing violently against the leather restraints. Even as Enrique rushed toward her, Rita propelled herself with such force that the straps on her gurney broke. The attendants summoned reinforcements and waved Enrique away. "Stay back," they warned.

"Rita, baby, I love you," Enrique called after her as she was wheeled through the emergency door. In the waiting room, he answered questions with growing impatience as the admitting nurse filled out official forms. A stout, gray-haired nurse took little Roberto from Maria. "We'll take care of the baby," she said gently.

Maria sighed with gratitude when Lonnie, Brett, and Sarah arrived. Lonnie sat down beside her on the vinyl couch and slipped his arm around her shoulder. He was still wearing his Hawaiian shirt, cutoffs and beach thongs. He clasped her hand as Enrique paced the floor, periodically demanding of a passing nurse, "When can I see my sister?"

"It may be quite a while," the admitting nurse told him finally. "Please go sit down, Mr. Fernandez."

"I'm going to wait here with Enrique no matter how long it takes," Maria told Lonnie. "You all can go home if you want."

"I'm staying with you, Maria," Lonnie assured her. "I want to see you through this."

"Why? It's not your problem."

"What—and who—you care about, Maria, I care about," Lonnie said, stroking her hair gently. "You ran away from me at the beach before we could talk. Did you really think what Lauren said would make a difference in my feelings for you?"

Maria's eyes were downcast. "I knew you'd be disappointed in me."

"It upset me, sure. I went through a lot of years of struggles and heartbreak with my dad. I know what alcohol or drug addiction can do to a person. But I learned a lot about love and understanding from my dad too. And if you need my help, Maria, I'm here for you."

"I smoked pot just one time, Lonnie. It really messed up my head. I realized right away that only Jesus could help me with my problems."

Sarah reached over and patted Maria's hand. "I'm here for you too, Maria. You can't get rid of your best friend just by running off from some old beach party."

Lonnie looked over at Enrique sitting hunched in a nearby chair. "Hey, buddy, if there's anything I can do to help, let me know, OK? I know what it's like to see someone you love strung out and hurting."

Enrique stared at Lonnie with wary, tear-rimmed eyes and muttered, "I don't need pity from no good-boy gringo."

Lonnie held Enrique's gaze. "Gringo? Yes. Good boy? Well, I'm not so sure. But listen, Enrique, it's not pity. I really want to help."

The reproach in Enrique's eyes dissolved. He massaged his jaw thoughtfully. "I hear you, man. Thanks."

They waited another half hour before the doctor—a lean, balding man with gold-rimmed spectacles—approached Enrique.

Enrique jumped up, his fists clenched. "How's Rita?"

The physician removed his glasses and wiped them on his lab coat. "We're doing our best, Mr. Fernandez."

"Will she be OK?"

"It's too soon to know. We found a combination of drugs in her system—cocaine, speed, PCP, angel dust. We can't be sure yet how they will affect her."

"What do you mean?" asked Enrique.

"Well, for example, PCP attacks a person at every level," the doctor replied. "It's a stimulant, a depressant, and an analgesic." He paused significantly, then continued. "It's also an anesthetic and a hallucinogen."

Enrique shook his head, baffled. "Those are big words," he complained. "I don't understand."

The doctor's brow furrowed. "Taking those drugs is like taking uppers, downers, alcohol, and acid all at once. The effect is volatile, devastating, and totally unpredictable."

"You saying Rita's going to end up crazy?"

"We don't know yet. These drugs cause memory loss and severe learning disabilities." The physician carefully replaced his glasses. "Only time will tell what brain damage has occurred in your sister."

"What about the baby?" asked Maria.

"We still have tests to run. From our cursory examination, I suspect there may be minimal brain dysfunction. Nevertheless, we're optimistic."

"I wanna see Rita," said Enrique.

"Not yet, Mr. Fernandez. She's heavily sedated." He looked over at Maria and Lonnie. "Why don't you go on home with your friends?"

"My friends?" echoed Enrique dubiously.

Lonnie stepped forward and put his hand on Enrique's shoulder. "Yes, Enrique," he said, "your friends."

Within the hour, they all went back to Enrique's house. His mother hadn't returned from work yet, but his younger brothers were already home demanding to know what had happened to Rita and little Roberto. While Enrique took them aside, Maria fixed hot chocolate, and Grandma Estrella brought over some sandwiches and oatmeal cookies. Enrique seemed reluctant at first to accept their offerings of food and sympathy, but gradually he warmed to their overtures of friendship and let down his guard.

After he had scooted his younger brothers off to bed, Enrique sat with one leg sprawled over the arm of his lumpy sofa and talked about life in the ghetto and his hopes for his family. "If— I mean, *when* Rita comes home, I like to see her find a husband and a father for little Roberto. I like to see my little brothers go to high school and get their diploma, and not quit like me. I don't want them being druggies and frying their brains like Rita done. And I wanna make enough bread so Mama don't have to clean toilets no more."

Maria and Sarah listened and nodded agreement with all of Enrique's hopes and dreams. Lonnie mentioned that he knew a construction company in Montebello that was hiring day laborers for good pay. He would get the number, and Enrique could give the guy a call. Brett said he might be able to come up with some good job leads Enrique and his mom could follow up too.

Finally Enrique looked up at the clock and said, "Hey, listen, dudes, I gotta call the hospital and see how Rita's doing."

While he went to he kitchen to make his call, Sarah turned to Maria and said, "I hope you don't mind, but I told Lonnie and Brett about what we saw at Denise's house that day. They agree that we should talk to our youth director. And they want to go with us."

"But what can Michael Dodd do?" asked Maria.

"I don't know. But it'll be a start. He'll have some ideas." Lonnie came over and sat down by Maria and took her hand. "What I've realized, Maria—what we've all got to realize—is that drugs aren't just a ghetto problem. The problem belongs to all of us. Rich guy, poor guy, Christian, non-Christian alike."

"And each of us is responsible for finding a solution," said Sarah. "We've got to help people realize that Jesus can fill the empty spaces in their lives. Drugs can't do that."

Maria nodded. "But how can we make people realize it's not just church or religion or even living a good life that makes a difference? It's getting to know Jesus as a real Person, as your Lord and Savior and best Friend. It's having His Spirit live in your heart that chases out the demons of drugs and fear and lone-liness. That's what I've discovered—the hard way.''

"OK, how do we get others to understand that?'' asked Lonnie.

"We do it by showing Jesus' love to other people,'' said Sarah.

"But where do we start?'' asked Brett. "So many people are throwing their lives away on drugs. Reaching them all is sta-tistically impossible and mentally overwhelming.''

Maria said softly, "I guess we do it one person at a time. Like we're doing tonight. Right now. With Enrique Fernandez.''

19

Two months later, just after school ended early in June, Maria packed for her trip to Colorado for her father's wedding. Reluctantly, Grandma Estrella agreed to go too. On the morning of their scheduled flight, Sarah stopped by with her twin brothers to say good-bye. Grandma Estrella led the boys to the kitchen for a handful of hard candy while the two girls chatted.

"So you're really going?" said Sarah wistfully, glancing at the luggage by the door.

Maria nodded. "Lonnie's driving us to the airport this afternoon."

"Are you excited?"

"I guess so." Maria chewed her lower lip. "I guess I'm a little scared too."

"Scared? Why?"

Maria unzipped her cosmetics bag and propped it open on the sofa. "What if Angela doesn't like me?"

"Oh, Maria, she'll love you!"

"I hope so. It's going to be so different, being part of a real family again."

"Then you've decided to stay in Colorado?"

"I don't know yet."

"Does Lonnie know you might not be back?"

"He says if I stay in Colorado, he might go to college in Denver just to be near me."

"That's what I call true love!" sighed Sarah.

Maria reached out and touched Sarah's hand. "I hate leaving you and Lonnie," she said, on the verge of tears. "I'm going to miss you both so much."

"Me too," sniffed Sarah. "Summer won't be the same without you."

Maria smiled ironically. "A few people like Lauren and Denise will be glad I'm gone."

For a long moment Sarah looked intently at Maria. "You've never really felt at home in our church, have you?"

Maria paused, reflecting. "No, I guess I haven't, but lately it doesn't bother me as much."

"How can it not bother you?"

"Because I've changed, Sarah. When I first came to California, I wanted so much to be accepted by everyone. Now I know that having a couple of loyal friends is more important than being popular or part of the in-crowd."

"I still feel bad about it," mused Sarah. "If our youth group had been more supportive, more caring, maybe this wouldn't have been such a painful year for you."

Maria thought about it, then said, "I came through OK, thanks to Jesus. Remember, He had only a handful of loyal friends too."

Sarah nodded. "You know, Michael Dodd is talking about starting some discipleship groups at church so we can learn how to help and encourage one another. And, of course, you already know about the support group he's started for kids coming off of drugs."

"That's a beginning, I guess," said Maria. "But nobody can make a person care for others unless that person chooses to."

"I care," said Sarah. "And I care about your friends Rita and Enrique too. How are they doing?"

Maria stuffed her shampoo bottle into her cosmetics bag. "They're doing OK so far," she replied. "Rita is in a drug therapy program at Metropolitan State Hospital in Norwalk."

"And Enrique?"

"I think his heart is opening to Jesus. In fact, he's started attending a little Latino church near here."

"I'm glad," said Sarah. She frowned mildly. "I don't suppose he'd consider coming to our church."

Maria shook her head. "Our church has a long way to go before people like Rita and Enrique—and me—really feel welcome."

Sarah pursed her lips thoughtfully. "Lonnie and Brett and I want to see what we can do to change that."

"If I come back to California, I'll help you too," said Maria.

Sarah glanced around the tidy little room. "Is your grandmother moving back to Colorado for good?"

"Oh, I wouldn't dare suggest such a thing to her," exclaimed Maria. "She says she's staying just for the wedding, then coming right back home, even if she has to hitchhike."

Sarah looked thoughtful. "Do you think she should live alone?"

"Not really," admitted Maria with a sigh. "Maybe I should come back with her. It's so hard to know what to do or where I really belong. I guess I'll just have to take one day at a time . . . and trust Jesus for the rest."

"That's the only way to go," smiled Sarah, a catch in her voice. She turned toward the kitchen. "I'd better get my brothers and get out of here so you can finish packing."

"Where are you going with the little rascals?"

"Crazy!" Sarah laughed. "No, really, I promised my mom I'd take them bowling."

"That sounds harmless enough."

"Harmless—are you kidding? Last time I took them bowling, Wally kept dropping the ball in the gutter. The finger holes were too big, so he stuffed them with bubble gum. Then Willie got his big toe stuck in his bowling ball. I called the manager over. He tried hot water, hand lotion, even bacon grease from the restaurant next door. Nothing worked, so finally he called the paramedics. I was mortified. Everyone in the bowling alley thought someone had died. Strangers tried to console me. I felt guilty telling them it was just a dumb bowling ball stuck on a little kid's fat toe."

Maria laughed. "I can just see Willie rolling around for the rest of his life with a bowling ball for a foot."

"Maybe he could get a job on one of those cranes with a ball and chain that destroys old buildings," giggled Sarah.

"Why not? He's already good at destroying things!" Maria was laughing so hard now her sides ached. She set her cosmetics bag beside her other luggage and went to Sarah for a hug. "Write me, Sarah," she said through her tears. "Tell me all about your brothers' crazy antics. Tell me about Lonnie and Brett and even Lauren's latest mischief. I don't want to feel cut off from everyone."

Weeping and laughing at once, Sarah held Maria at arms' length and said, "Tell yourself, 'I am embarking on the adventure of my life!'"

Maria wiped her eyes and summoned her most dignified voice. "I am embarking on the adventure of my life!" She and Sarah embraced again and laughed. As their merriment subsided and their tears fell unashamedly, Maria felt better somehow, refreshed, reassured. She wished she could find the words to tell Sarah how she felt. It was going to be hard starting over, making new friends, finding her niche in her new family. But she wasn't alone. She understood that at last. She had Jesus. She had a precious handful of people who loved her. What more could anyone ask for?